THE HAUNTED MASK II

Look for other **Goosebumps** books
by R.L. Stine:

The Abominable Snowman of Pasadena
Attack of The Mutant
Bad Hare Day
The Barking Ghost
The Cuckoo Clock of Doom
The Curse of the Mummy's Tomb
Deep Trouble
Egg Monsters From Mars
Ghost Beach
Ghost Camp
The Ghost Next Door
Go Eat Worms!
The Haunted Mask
The Headless Ghost
The Horror at Camp Jellyjam
How I Got My Shrunken Head
How to Kill a Monster
It Came From Beneath the Sink!
Let's Get Invisible!
Monster Blood
Monster Blood II
A Night in Terror Tower
Night of the Living Dummy
Night of the Living Dummy II
One Day at HorrorLand
Piano Lessons Can Be Murder
Revenge of the Lawn Gnomes
Say Cheese and Die!
Say Cheese and Die . . . Again!
The Scarecrow Walks at Midnight
A Shocker on Shock Street
Stay Out of the Basement
Welcome to Camp Nightmare
Welcome to Dead House
The Werewolf of Fever Swamp
You Can't Scare Me!

Goosebumps®

THE HAUNTED MASK II

R.L. STINE

SCHOLASTIC INC.
New York Toronto London Auckland Sydney
Mexico City New Delhi Hong Kong Buenos Aires

ISBN 0-439-67113-2

The *Goosebumps* book series created by Parachute Press, Inc.
Published by Scholastic Inc.
SCHOLASTIC, GOOSEBUMPS, and associated logos are trademarks and/or registered trademarks of Scholastic Inc.

12 11 10 9 8 7 6 5 4 3 2 '   4 5 6 7 8 9/0

Printed in the U.S.A.   40

1

I don't know if you have ever spent any time with first graders. But there is only one word to describe them. And that word is ANIMALS.

First graders are animals.

You can quote me.

My name is Steve Boswell, and I am in the sixth grade. I may not be the smartest guy at Walnut Avenue Middle School. But I know one thing for sure: First graders are animals.

How do I know this fact? I learned it the hard way. I learned it by coaching the first-grade soccer team after school every day.

You might want to know *why* I chose to coach their soccer team. Well, I didn't *choose* it. It was a punishment.

Someone set a squirrel loose in the girls' locker room. That someone was me. But it wasn't my idea.

My best friend, Chuck Greene, caught the squirrel. And he asked me where I thought he should set it free.

I said, "How about the girls' locker room before their basketball game on Thursday?"

So maybe it was partly my idea. But Chuck was just as much to blame as I was.

Of course, I was the one who got caught.

Miss Curdy, the gym teacher, grabbed me as I was letting the squirrel out of its box. The squirrel ran across the gym to the bleachers. The kids in the bleachers all jumped up and started running and screaming and acting crazy.

It was just a dumb squirrel. But all the teachers started chasing after it. It took hours to catch it and get everyone calmed down.

So Miss Curdy said I had to be punished.

She gave me a choice of punishments. One: I could come into the gym after school every day and inflate basketballs — by mouth — until my head exploded. Or two: I could coach the first-grade soccer team.

I chose number two.

The wrong choice.

My friend Chuck was supposed to help me coach the team. But he told Miss Curdy he had an after-school job.

Do you know what his after-school job is? Going home and watching TV.

A lot of people think that Chuck and I are best friends because we look so much alike. We're both

2

tall and thin. We both have straight brown hair and dark brown eyes. We both wear baseball caps most of the time. Sometimes people think we're brothers!

But that's not why I like Chuck and Chuck likes me. We're best friends because we make each other laugh.

I laughed really hard when Chuck told me what his after-school job was. But I'm not laughing now.

I'm praying. Every day I pray for rain. If it rains, the first graders don't have soccer practice.

Today, unfortunately, is a bright, clear, beautiful October day. Standing on the playground behind school, I searched the sky for a cloud — any cloud — but saw only blue.

"Okay, listen up, Hogs!" I shouted. I wasn't making fun of them. That's the name they voted for their team. Do you believe it? The Walnut Avenue Hogs.

Does that give you an idea of what these kids are like?

I cupped my hands around my mouth and shouted again. "Line up, Hogs!"

Andrew Foster grabbed the whistle I wear around my neck and blew it in my face. Then Duck Benton tromped down hard on my new sneakers. Everyone calls him Duck because he quacks all the time. He and Andrew thought that was a riot.

3

Then Marnie Rosen jumped up behind me, threw her arms around my neck, and climbed on my back. Marnie has curly red hair, freckles all over her face, and the most evil grin I ever saw on a kid. "Give me a ride, Steve!" she shouted. "I want a ride!"

"Marnie — get off me!" I cried. I tried to loosen her grip on my neck. She was *choking* me. The Hogs were all laughing now.

"Marnie — I . . . can't . . . breathe!" I gasped.

I bent down and tried to throw her off my back. But she hung on even tighter.

Then I felt her lips press against my ear.

"What are you *doing*?" I cried. Was she trying to kiss me or something?

Yuck! She spit her bubble gum into my ear.

Then, laughing like a crazed fiend, she hopped off me and went running across the grass, her curly red hair bouncing behind her.

"Give me a *break*!" I cried angrily. The purple gum stuck in my ear. It took me a while to scrape it all out.

By the time I finished, they had started a practice game.

Have you ever watched six-year-olds play soccer? It's chase and kick, chase and kick. Everybody chase the ball. Everybody try to kick it.

I try to teach them positions. I try to teach them how to pass the ball to each other. I try to teach

4

them teamwork. But all they want to do is chase and kick, chase and kick.

Which is fine with me. As long as they leave me alone.

I blow my whistle and act as umpire. And try to keep the game going.

Andrew Foster kicked a big clump of dirt on my jeans as he ran by. He acted as if it were an accident. But I knew it was deliberate.

Then Duck Benton got into a shoving fight with Johnny Myers. Duck watches hockey games on TV with his dad, and he thinks you're *supposed* to fight. Some days Duck doesn't chase after the ball at all. He just fights.

I let them chase-and-kick, chase-and-kick for an hour. Then I blew the whistle to call practice to an end.

Not a bad practice. Only one bloody nose. And that was a win because it wasn't mine!

"Okay, Hogs — see you tomorrow!" I shouted. I started to trot off the playground. Their parents or baby-sitters would be waiting for them in front of the school.

Then I saw that a bunch of the kids had formed a tight circle in the middle of the field. They all wore grins on their faces, so I decided I'd better see what they were up to.

"What's going on, guys?" I asked, trotting back to them.

Some kids stepped back, and I spotted a soccer ball on the grass. Marnie Rosen smiled at me through her freckles. "Hey, Steve, can you kick a goal from here?"

The other kids stepped away from the ball. I glanced to the goal. It was really far away, at least half the field.

"What's the joke?" I demanded.

Marnie's grin faded. "No joke. Can you kick a goal from here?"

"No way!" Duck Benton called.

"Steve can do it," I heard Johnny Myers say. "Steve can kick it farther than that."

"No way!" Duck insisted. "It's too far even for a sixth grader."

"Hey — that's an easy goal," I bragged. "Why don't you give me something *hard* to do?"

Every once in a while I have to do something to impress them. Just to prove that I'm better than they are.

So I moved up behind the ball. I stopped about eight or ten steps back. Gave myself plenty of running room.

"Okay, guys, watch how a pro does it!" I cried.

I ran up to the ball. Got plenty of leg behind it.

Gave a tremendous kick.

Froze for a second.

And then let out a long, high wail of horror.

2

On my way home a few minutes later, I passed my friend Chuck's house. Chuck came running down the gravel driveway to greet me.

I didn't really feel like talking to anyone. Not even my friend.

But there he was. So what could I do?

"Yo — Steve!" He stopped halfway down the driveway. "What happened? Why are you limping?"

"Concrete," I groaned.

He pulled off his black-and-red Cubs cap and scratched his thick brown hair. "Huh?"

"Concrete," I repeated weakly. "The kids had a concrete soccer ball."

Chuck squinted at me. I could see he still didn't understand.

"One of the kids lives across the street. He had his friends help roll a ball of concrete to the school," I explained. "Painted white and black to look like a soccer ball. Solid concrete. They had it there on the field. They asked me to kick a goal and — and — " My voice caught in my throat. I couldn't finish.

I hobbled over to the big beech tree beside Chuck's driveway and leaned back against its cold, white trunk.

"Wow. That's not a very funny joke," Chuck said, replacing his cap on his head.

"Tell me about it," I groaned. "I think I broke every bone in my foot. Even some bones I don't have."

"Those kids are *animals!*" Chuck declared.

I groaned and rubbed my aching foot. It wasn't really broken. But it hurt. A lot. I shifted my backpack on my shoulders and leaned back against the tree.

"Know what I'd like to do?" I told Chuck.

"Pay them back?"

"You're right!" I replied. "How did you know?"

"Lucky guess." He stepped up beside me. I could see that he was thinking hard. Chuck always scrunches up his face when he's trying to think.

"It's almost Halloween," he said finally. "Maybe we could think of some way to scare them. I mean, *really* scare them." His dark eyes lit up with excitement.

"Well . . . maybe." I hesitated. "They're just little kids. I don't want to do anything mean."

My backpack felt weird — too full. I pulled it off my shoulder and lowered it to the ground.

I leaned over and unzipped it.

And about ten million feathers came floating out.

"Those kids — !" Chuck exclaimed.

I pulled open the backpack. All of my notebooks, all of my textbooks — covered in sticky feathers. Those animals had glued feathers to my books.

I tossed down the backpack and turned to Chuck. "Maybe I *do* want to do something mean!" I growled.

A few days later, Chuck and I were walking home from the playground. It was a cold, windy afternoon. Dark storm clouds rose up in the distance.

The storm clouds were too late to help me. I had just finished afternoon practice with the Hogs.

It hadn't been a bad practice. It hadn't been a *good* practice, either.

Just as we started, Andrew Foster lowered his head and came at me full speed. He weighs about a thousand pounds, and he has a very hard head. He plowed into my stomach and knocked the wind out of me.

I rolled around on the ground for a few minutes, groaning and choking and gasping. The kids thought it was pretty funny. Andrew claimed it was an accident.

I'm going to get you guys back, I vowed to myself. *I don't know how. But I'm going to get you guys.*

Then Marnie Rosen jumped on my back and tore the collar off my new winter coat.

Chuck met me after practice. He'd started doing that now. He knew that after one hour with the first graders, I usually needed help getting home.

"I hate them," I muttered. "Do you know how to spell hate? H–O–G–S." My torn coat collar flapped in the swirling wind.

"Why don't you make all of them practice with a concrete ball?" Chuck suggested. He adjusted his Cubs cap over his hair. "No. Wait. I've got it. Let them take turns *being* the ball!"

"No. No good," I replied, shaking my head. The sky darkened. The trees shook, sending a shower of dead leaves down around us.

My sneakers crunched over the leaves. "I don't want to hurt them," I told Chuck. "I just want to scare them. I just want to scare them to death."

The wind blew colder. I felt a cold drop of rain on my forehead.

As we crossed the street, I noticed two girls from our class walking on the other side. I recognized Sabrina Mason's black ponytail swinging behind her as she hurried along the sidewalk. And next to her, I recognized her friend Carly Beth Caldwell.

10

"Hey — !" I started to call out to them, but I stopped.

An idea flashed into my mind.

Seeing Carly Beth, I knew how to scare those first graders.

Seeing Carly Beth, I knew exactly what I wanted to do.

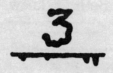

3

I started to call to the girls. But Chuck clamped his hand over my mouth and dragged me behind a wide tree.

"Hey — get your clammy paws off me. What's the big idea?" I cried when he finally pulled his hand away.

He pushed me against the rough bark of the tree trunk. "Ssshhh. They haven't seen us." He motioned with his eyes toward the two girls.

"So?"

"So we can sneak up and scare them," Chuck whispered, his dark eyes practically glowing with evil excitement. "Let's make Carly Beth scream."

"You mean for old times' sake?"

Chuck nodded, grinning.

For many years, making Carly Beth scream had been our hobby. That's because she was a really good screamer, and she would scream at just about anything.

One day in the lunchroom last year, Chuck

tucked a worm inside his turkey sandwich. Then he gave the sandwich to Carly Beth.

She took one bite and knew that something tasted a little weird. When Chuck showed her the big bite she had taken out of the worm, Carly Beth screamed for a week.

Chuck and I took bets on who could scare Carly Beth the most and who could make her scream. I guess it was kind of mean. But it was funny too.

And sometimes when you know that people are real easy to scare, you have no choice. You *have* to scare them as often as you can.

Anyway, that all changed last Halloween.

Last Halloween Chuck and I had a horrible scare. Carly Beth wore the most frightening mask I had ever seen. It wasn't a mask. It was like a living face.

It was so ugly, so real. It glared at us with evil, living eyes. Its mouth sneered at us with real lips. The skin glowed a sick green. And Carly Beth's normally soft voice burst out in a terrifying animal growl.

Chuck and I ran for our lives.

No joke. We were terrified.

We ran for blocks, screaming the whole way. It was the worst night of my life.

Everything changed after that.

Nearly a whole year has gone by, and we haven't tried to scare Carly Beth once. I don't think Carly Beth *can* be scared. Not anymore.

After last Halloween, I don't think anything scares her.

She is totally fearless. I haven't heard her shriek or scream once the entire year.

So I didn't want to try to scare her now. I needed to talk to her. About that scary mask of hers.

But Chuck kept pressing me back against the tree trunk. "Come on, Steve," he whispered. "They don't see us. We'll duck down behind the hedges and get ahead of them. Then when they come by, we'll jump out and grab them."

"I don't really — " I started. But I could see that Chuck had his heart set on scaring Carly Beth and Sabrina. So I let him pull me down out of sight.

A light rain had started to fall. The gusting wind blew the raindrops into my face. I crept along the hedge, bent low, following Chuck.

We passed by the girls and kept moving. I could hear Sabrina's laugh behind us. I heard Carly Beth say something else. Then Sabrina laughed again.

I wondered what they were talking about. I stopped to glance through the hedge. Carly Beth had a weird expression on her face. Her dark eyes stared straight ahead. She was moving stiffly. She had the collar of her blue down jacket pulled up high around her face.

I ducked down low again as the girls came closer. I turned and saw that Chuck and I were standing on the wide front lawn of the old Carpenter mansion.

I felt a chill as I stared across the weed-choked lawn at the gloomy old house, covered in a deep darkness. Everyone said that the house was haunted — haunted by people who had been murdered inside it a hundred years ago.

I don't believe in ghosts. But I don't like standing so close to the creepy old Carpenter mansion, either.

I pulled Chuck into the empty lot next door. Rain pattered the ground. I wiped raindrops off my eyebrows.

Carly Beth and Sabrina were only a few yards away. I could hear Sabrina talking excitedly about something. But I couldn't make out her words.

Chuck turned to me, an evil grin spreading across his face. "Ready?" he whispered. "Let's get 'em!"

We leaped to our feet. Then we both jumped out, screaming at the top of our lungs.

Sabrina gasped in shock. Her mouth dropped to her knees. Her hands flew up in the air.

Carly Beth stared at me.

Then her head tilted against the blue jacket collar — tilted and fell.

Her head fell off her shoulders.

It dropped to the ground and bounced onto the grass.

Sabrina lowered her eyes to the ground. She gaped at Carly Beth's fallen head in disbelief.

Then Sabrina's hands began to flail the air crazily. She opened her mouth in a scream of horror. And screamed and screamed and screamed.

4

I swallowed hard. My knees started to buckle.

Carly Beth's head stared up at me from the grass. Sabrina's shrieks rang in my ears.

And then I heard soft laughter. Laughter from inside Carly Beth's jacket.

I saw a clump of brown hair poke up through the raised collar. And then Carly Beth's laughing face shot up from under the jacket.

Sabrina stopped her wild cries and started to laugh.

"Gotcha!" Carly Beth cried. She and Sabrina fell all over each other, laughing like lunatics.

"Oh, wow," Chuck groaned.

My knees were still shaking. I don't think I had taken a breath the whole time.

I bent down and picked up Carly Beth's head. Some kind of dummy head. A sculpture, I guess. I rolled it around between my hands. It was amazing. It looked just like her.

"It's plaster of Paris," Carly Beth explained,

grabbing it away from me. "My mom made it."

"But — it's so real-looking!" I choked out.

She grinned. "Mom is getting pretty good. She keeps doing my head over and over. This is one of her best."

"It's okay. But it didn't fool us," Chuck said.

"Yeah. We knew it was a fake," I quickly agreed. But my voice cracked when I said it. I was still kind of in shock.

Sabrina shook her head. Her black ponytail waved behind her. Sabrina is very tall, taller than Chuck and me. Carly Beth is a shrimp. She only comes up to Sabrina's shoulder.

"You should have seen the looks on your faces!" Sabrina exclaimed. "I thought *your* heads were going to fall off!"

The two girls hugged each other again and had another good laugh.

"We saw you a mile away," Carly Beth said, twirling the head in her hands. "Luckily, I brought this head in to show off in art class today. So I pulled my jacket over my head, and Sabrina tucked the plaster head into the collar."

"You guys scare pretty easy," Sabrina smirked.

"We *weren't* scared. Really," Chuck insisted. "We were just playing along."

I wanted to change the subject. The girls would talk all day and night about how dumb Chuck and I were. If we let them. I didn't want to let them.

The rain kept pattering down, blown by the

18

gusting wind. I shivered. We were all getting pretty wet.

"Carly Beth, you know that mask you wore last Halloween? Where did you get it?" I asked. I tried to sound casual. I didn't want her to think it was any big deal.

She hugged her plaster head against the front of her jacket. "Huh? What mask?"

I groaned. She is such a jerk sometimes!

"Remember that really scary mask you had last Halloween? Where did you get it?"

She and Sabrina exchanged glances. Then Carly Beth said, "I don't remember."

"Give me a break!" I groaned.

"No. Really — " she insisted.

"You remember," Chuck told her. "You just don't want to tell."

I knew why Carly Beth didn't want to tell. She was probably planning to get another truly terrifying mask at the same store for this Halloween. She wanted to be the scariest kid in town. She didn't want me to be scary too.

I turned to Sabrina. "Do you know where she bought that mask?"

Sabrina made a zipper motion over her lips. "I'm not telling, Steve."

"You don't want to know," Carly Beth declared, still hugging the head. "That mask was *too* frightening."

"You just want to be scarier than me," I replied

19

angrily. "But I need a really scary mask this year, Carly Beth. There are some kids I want to scare and — "

"I'm serious, Steve," Carly Beth interrupted. "There was something totally weird about the mask. It wasn't just a mask. It came alive. It clamped onto my head, and I couldn't get it off. The mask was haunted or something."

"Ha-ha," I said, rolling my eyes.

"She's telling the truth!" Sabrina cried, narrowing her dark eyes at me.

"The mask was evil," Carly Beth continued. "It started giving me orders. It started talking all by itself, in a horrible, harsh growl. I couldn't control it. And I couldn't get it off. It was attached to my head! I — I was so scared!"

"Oh, wow," Chuck murmured, shaking his head. "You've got a good imagination, Carly Beth."

"Good story," I agreed. "Save it for English class."

"But it's the *truth!*" Carly Beth cried.

"You just don't want me to be scary," I grumbled. "But I need a good, scary mask like that one. Come on," I begged. "Tell."

"Tell us," Chuck insisted.

"Tell," I repeated, trying to sound tough.

"No way," Carly Beth replied, shaking her fake round, little head. "Let's get home. It's really raining hard."

"Not till you tell!" I cried. I stepped in front of her to block her path.

"Grab the head!" Chuck cried.

I grabbed the plaster head from Carly Beth's hands.

"Give it back!" she shrieked. She swiped at it, but I swung it out of her reach. Then I tossed it to Chuck.

He backed away. Sabrina chased after him. "Give that back to her!"

"We'll give it back when you tell us where you bought that mask!" I told Carly Beth.

"No way!" she cried.

Chuck tossed the head to me. Carly Beth made a wild grab for it. But I caught it and heaved it back to Chuck.

"Give it back! Come on!" Carly Beth cried, running after Chuck. "My mom made that. If it gets messed up, she'll *kill* me!"

"Then tell me where you bought the mask!" I insisted.

Chuck tossed the head to me. Sabrina jumped up and batted it down. She made a wild dive for it, but I got there first. I picked it up off the grass and heaved it back to Chuck.

"Stop it! Give it back!"

Both girls were screaming angrily. But Chuck and I kept up our game of keep-away.

Carly Beth made a frantic leap for the head and fell on her stomach onto the grass. When she stood up, the front of her jacket and her jeans were soaked, and she had grass stains on her forehead.

"Tell!" I insisted, holding the head high in the air. "Tell, and you can have the head back!"

She growled at me.

"Okay," I warned her. "I guess I have to drop-kick it onto that roof."

I turned toward the house at the top of the lawn. Then I held the head in front of me in both hands and pretended I was going to punt it onto the roof.

"Okay, okay!" Carly Beth cried. "Don't kick it, Steve."

I kept the head in front of me. "Where did you get the mask?"

"You know that weird little party store a couple of blocks from school?"

I nodded. I had seen the store, but I had never gone in.

"That's where I bought it. There's a back room. It was filled with weird, ugly masks. That's where I got mine."

"All right!" I cried happily. I handed Carly Beth back her head.

"You guys are creeps," Sabrina muttered, pulling her collar up against the rain. She pushed me out of the way and wiped the grass stain off Carly Beth's forehead.

"I really didn't want to tell you," Carly Beth moaned. "I wasn't making that story up about the mask. It was so terrifying."

"Yeah. Sure." I rolled my eyes again.

"Please, don't go there!" Carly Beth begged. She grabbed my arm tightly. "Please, Steve. Please, don't go to that party store!"

I pulled my arm away. I narrowed my eyes at her. And I laughed.

Too bad I didn't take her seriously.

Too bad I didn't listen to her.

It might have saved me from a night of endless horror.

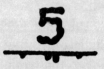

5

"Get off me! Get off me, Marnie! I *mean* it!" I shouted.

The little redheaded pest hung onto my back, laughing and digging her pudgy fingers into my neck. Why did she think I was some kind of thrill ride?

"Get off! This is my good sweater!" I cried. "If you wreck it — "

She laughed even harder.

It had rained all night and all morning. But the clouds had parted at lunchtime. Now the sky was blue and clear. I had no choice. I had to hold soccer practice for the Hogs.

Across the playground, I saw Duck Benton fighting with Andrew Foster. Andrew picked up the soccer ball and heaved it with all his might into Duck's stomach.

Duck's mouth shot open. He let out a whoosh of breath, and a huge wad of bubblegum went flying into the air.

"Get off!" I pleaded with Marnie. I tried spinning and twirling as fast as I could, trying to throw her off my back. I knew if anything happened to this sweater, Mom would have a fit.

You might ask why I was wearing my best, blue wool sweater to soccer practice. Good question.

The answer is: It was Class Photo Day. And Mom wanted me to take a really good picture to send to all my aunts and uncles. She made me wear the sweater. And she made me shampoo my hair before school and not wear my Orlando Magic cap over it.

So I looked like a jerk all day. And now, here was soccer practice. And I had forgotten to bring a sweatshirt or something to replace my good sweater.

"Whoooooa!" Marnie gave me a final kick in the side as she hopped off my back.

I pulled down my sweater, hoping it wasn't stretched too badly. I heard angry shouts and glanced up to find Andrew and Duck swinging their fists at each other and butting heads across the field.

I reached for my whistle.

And grabbed air.

Marnie had swiped it. She held it high above her head and ran, laughing, over the grass.

"Hey, you — !" I screamed, chasing after the little thief.

I took three steps — and my sneakers slid in

the mud. My feet flew out from under me. With an angry cry, I fell forward. And landed on my stomach in deep, wet mud.

"Noooooo!" I let out a howl of dread. "Please. Nooooo!"

But when I pulled myself up, the mud came with me. My entire body was caked in thick, wet mud. My beautiful blue sweater? It was now an ugly *brown* sweater.

With a sad groan, I sank back onto the ground. I just wanted to disappear, to sink from sight into the big mud hole.

My faithful team, the Horrible Hogs, were laughing and hooting. They thought it was a riot. Nice kids, huh?

At least my mud dive had stopped Andrew and Duck from fighting.

The mud weighed me down as I climbed slowly to my feet. I felt like Andrew. I felt as if I weighed a thousand pounds. Maybe I did!

I wiped mud off my eyes with both hands — and saw Chuck standing over me. He tsk-tsked a few times. "You look really bad, man."

"Tell me something I don't know," I muttered.

"Why did you do that?" he asked.

I squinted through two inches of mud at him. "Excuse me?"

"You look like Mud Monster or something." Chuck snickered.

"Ha-ha," I said glumly.

"You told me to meet you here, Steve. You said we were going straight to that party store to buy the you-know-what."

He glanced back at my team of first graders. They weren't listening to our conversation. They were too busy flinging mud balls at each other.

I scooped my hand along the front of my sweater and scraped off about ten pounds of glop. "I . . . uh . . . I think I'd better go home after practice and get changed first," I told Chuck.

Talk about your *long* afternoons!

I had to break up the mud ball fight. Then I had to hand over all of the little angels to their parents and baby-sitters.

Then I had to explain to their angry parents and baby-sitters why they had practiced mud ball fighting instead of soccer.

I crept home. Chuck waited for me outside. I hid my mud-caked clothes in the back of my closet. I didn't have time to explain to my mom.

Then I changed into a clean pair of jeans and a gray-and-red Georgetown Hoyas sweatshirt one of my uncles had sent me. I don't know anything about the Hoyas. I don't even know what a Hoya is. But it is a cool sweatshirt.

I pulled my cap down over my mud-drenched hair. Then I hurried to meet Chuck.

"Steve — is that you?" Mom called from the den.

"No, it isn't!" I called back. I closed the front door behind me and ran down the driveway before she could stop me from going out again.

I was really eager to find that party store and check out the weird masks. So eager, I forgot to bring any money with me.

Chuck and I walked two blocks before I reached into my jeans pocket and realized it was empty. We jogged back to my house, and I crept up to my room once again.

"This just isn't my day," I muttered to myself.

But I knew that buying a really gross and frightening mask would instantly cheer me up. Then I could go ahead with my plan to terrify the Hogs, to get my revenge.

Revenge!

What a beautiful word.

When I'm older and have my own car, that's what I want it to say on my license plate.

I pulled all of my allowance money out of the dresser drawer where I hide it. I counted it quickly — about twenty-five dollars. Then I jammed the bills into my jeans pocket and hurried back downstairs.

"Steve — are you going out again?" Mom called from the den.

"Be right back!" I shouted. I slammed the front door and ran down the driveway to meet Chuck.

Our sneakers slid over fat, wet leaves as we walked. A pale full moon hung low over the trees.

The streets and sidewalks still glistened from all the rain.

Chuck had his hands stuffed into the pockets of his hooded sweatshirt. He leaned into the wind as we walked. "I'm going to be late for dinner," he grumbled. "I'm probably going to get into major trouble."

"It'll be worth it," I told him, feeling a little more cheerful. We crossed the street that led to the party store. A small grocery stood on the corner. Other small shops came into view.

"I can't wait to see these masks!" I exclaimed. "If I find one just *half* as scary as Carly Beth's . . ."

There it stood! In the darkness above a small, square store, I could make out the sign: THE PARTY PLACE.

"Let's check it out!" I cried.

I leaped over a fire hydrant.

Flew over the sidewalk. Up to the big front window.

And peered in the window.

6

"Oh, wow!" Chuck cried breathlessly, stepping up beside me.

We both pressed our faces against the window glass and stared in.

Stared into total darkness.

"Is it closed?" Chuck asked softly. "Maybe it's just closed for the night."

I uttered an unhappy sigh. "No way. It's closed for good. The store is gone."

Peering through the dust-smeared glass, I could see empty shelves and display racks inside. A tall metal shelf lay on its side across the center aisle. A trash basket, overflowing with paper and empty soda cans, stood on top of the counter.

"There's no 'Out of Business' sign on the door," Chuck said. He's a good friend. He saw how disappointed I looked. He was trying to stay hopeful.

"It's empty." I sighed. "Totally cleaned out. It isn't going to open up again tomorrow morning."

"Yeah. Guess you're right," Chuck murmured.

He slapped my shoulder. "Yo — snap out of it. You'll find a scary mask at some other store."

I pushed myself away from the window. "I wanted one like Carly Beth's," I complained. "You remember that mask. You remember those glowing eyes, right? And the way the mouth moved. The way it growled at us with those long, dripping fangs. It was so gross. And it looked totally real. Like a real monster!"

"They probably have masks like that at K-Mart," Chuck said.

"Give me a break," I muttered. I kicked at a candy wrapper that blew across the sidewalk.

A car rumbled past slowly. Its headlights rolled over the front of the store, lighting up the bare shelves, the empty counters inside.

"We'd better get home," Chuck warned, pulling me away from the store. "I'm not allowed to wander around town after dark."

He said something else, but I didn't hear him. I was still picturing Carly Beth's mask, still unable to get over my disappointment.

"You don't understand how important this is to me," I told Chuck. "Those first graders are ruining my life. I have to pay them back this Halloween. I have to."

"They're just first graders," he replied.

"No, they're not. They're monsters. Vicious, man-eating monsters."

"Maybe we can *make* a scary mask," Chuck

suggested. "You know. Out of papier-mâché and stuff."

I didn't even bother to answer him. Chuck is a good guy, but sometimes he has the dumbest ideas ever thought up by a human.

I could just see Marnie Rosen and Duck Benton when I popped out on Halloween. *"Ooh, we're scared! We're scared! Papier-mâché!"*

"I'm hungry," Chuck grumbled. "Come on, Steve. Let's get out of here."

"Yeah. Okay," I agreed. I started to follow him down the sidewalk — then stopped.

Another car had turned onto the street. Its headlights rolled over a narrow alley beside the party store.

"Whoa, Chuck! Check it out!" I grabbed the shoulder of his sweatshirt and spun him around. "Look!" I pointed into the alley. "That door is open!"

"Huh? What door?"

I dragged Chuck into the alley. A large black trapdoor in the sidewalk had been left up. It caught the light from a streetlamp on the sidewalk.

Chuck and I peered in through the door. Steep concrete steps led down to a basement.

The basement of the party store!

Chuck turned to me, a confused expression on his face. "So? They left the basement door open. So what?"

I grabbed the open trapdoor and leaned over the steps, squinting into the dim light from the streetlamp. "There are boxes down there. A whole bunch of cartons."

He still didn't understand.

"Maybe all the masks and costumes and party things are packed up in those cartons. Maybe the stuff hasn't been shipped away yet."

"Whoa. What are you thinking about?" Chuck demanded. "You're not going down there — are you? You're not going to sneak down to that dark basement and try to steal a mask — *are you?*"

I didn't answer him.

I was already halfway down the stairs.

7

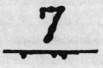

My heart began to pound as I made my way down. The steps were narrow and slippery. Slick from all the rain.

"Ohh!" I let out a cry as one foot slid over the concrete step and I felt myself start to fall. I shot out both hands in search of a railing — but there wasn't one.

I landed on the hard basement floor with a loud *thud* — luckily, on both feet. Feeling shaken, I took a deep breath and held it.

Then I turned back to the trapdoor and called up to Chuck. "I'm okay. Get down here."

In the light from the streetlamp, I could see his unhappy face peering down at me. "I — I really don't want to," he called softly.

"Chuck — hurry," I insisted. "Get out of the alley. If someone drives by and sees you, they'll get suspicious."

"But it's so late, Steve," he whined. "And it isn't right to break into basements and — "

"We're not breaking in," I called up to him impatiently. "The door was open — right? Hurry up. If the two of us search the boxes, we can do it in five minutes."

He leaned down over the opening. "It's too dark," he complained. "We don't have a flashlight or anything."

"I can see fine," I replied. "Get down here. You're wasting time."

"But it's against the law . . ." he started. Then I saw his expression change. His mouth dropped open as car headlights washed over him. With a low gasp, Chuck ducked through the opening, and bolted down the stairs.

He stepped up close beside me, breathing hard. "I don't think they saw me." His eyes darted around the large basement. "It's too dark, Steve. Let's go home."

"Give your eyes a chance to adjust," I instructed him. "I can see okay."

I gazed slowly around the basement. It was bigger than I'd thought. I couldn't really see the walls. They were hidden in darkness.

The ceiling was low, only a foot or two over our heads. Even in the dim light, I could see the thick cobwebs in the rafters.

The cartons had been stacked in two rows near the steps. Somewhere way across the room, I could hear the steady *drip drip drip* of water.

"Oh!" I jumped when I heard a clattering sound.

It took me a few seconds to figure out that it was the wind blowing against the metal trapdoor up in the alley.

I made my way over to the nearest carton and bent over to examine it. The flaps were folded over each other. But the carton wasn't sealed.

"Let's have a look," I murmured, reaching for the flaps.

Chuck had his arms crossed tightly in front of his chest. "This isn't right," he protested. "It's stealing."

"We haven't taken anything," I protested. "And even if we do find a good, scary mask and take it, we'll just borrow it. We'll return it after Halloween."

"Aren't you . . . a little scared?" Chuck asked softly, his eyes moving all around the dark room.

I nodded. "Yeah. I'm a little scared," I admitted. "It's cold and creepy down here." The wind clattered the trapdoor above us again. I heard the faint *drip* of water against the concrete floor.

"Let's hurry," I urged. "Help me."

Chuck stepped beside me, but he just stared down at the box and didn't try to help.

I pulled open the first carton, pushed back the cardboard flaps, and peered inside. "What *is* this stuff?" I reached in and pulled out a cone-shaped party hat. The box was stuffed with party hats.

"This is great!" I whispered happily to Chuck.

I dropped the hat back in the box. "I was right. All the stuff from the store is packed up down here. We're going to find the scary masks. I know we will!"

Cartons were stacked on top of cartons. I pulled down another one and started to pull it open. "Chuck, you take the bottom one," I instructed.

He hesitantly reached for the box. "I have a bad feeling about this, Steve," he murmured.

"Just find the masks," I replied. My heart was thudding. My hands were shaking as I pulled open the second carton. I was really excited.

"This one is filled with candles," Chuck reported.

My carton had piles of party place mats, napkins, and paper cups. "Keep going," I urged. "The masks have got to be down here."

Above our heads, the wind shook the trapdoor. I hoped it wouldn't suddenly slam shut on us. I didn't want to be trapped down in this cold basement in the dark.

Chuck and I slid two more cartons into the pale square of light from outside. My carton was taped shut. I struggled to pull off the tape.

I stopped when I heard the creaking sound above my head.

Creaking floorboards?

I froze, my hands over the carton. "What was that?" I whispered.

Chuck frowned at me. "What was what?"

"Didn't you hear that noise upstairs? It sounded like a footstep."

Chuck shook his head. "I didn't hear anything."

I listened for a few more seconds. Silence now. So I went back to work on the carton.

I pulled it open and peered eagerly inside.

Greeting cards. Dozens of greeting cards. I sifted through them. Birthday cards. Valentines. A whole carton of cards.

Disappointed, I shoved the carton to the side and turned to Chuck. "Any luck?"

"Not yet. Let's see what's in this one."

He pulled open the carton with both hands. Then he leaned over it and peered inside.

"Oh, *yuck!*" he cried.

"It's so gross!" Chuck groaned.

"What is? What?" I demanded. I leaped over my carton to get to him.

"Check it out." A grin spread over Chuck's face as he pulled something out of the carton.

I gasped as I saw an ugly purple face with broken teeth and a long, fat worm poking out of a hole in its cheek.

"You found them!" I shrieked.

Chuck let out a gleeful laugh. "A whole carton of masks! And they're all totally gross!"

I grabbed the ugly mask from his hand and studied it. "Hey — it feels warm!"

It was so cold down in that basement. Why did the mask feel warm?

The worm bobbed out of the ugly face, as if it were alive.

I dropped the mask, plunged my hand into the carton, and pulled out another one. A disgusting

39

pig face with thick gobs of green stuff dripping from its snout.

"That one looks like Carly Beth!" Chuck joked.

"These are scarier than the mask Carly Beth had last year," I said.

I pulled another one from the box. A furry animal face, sort of like a gorilla, except that it had two long pointed fangs sliding down past its chin.

I dropped it and grabbed up another mask. Then another. A hideous bald head with one eye hanging down by a thread and an arrow through the forehead.

I tossed it to Chuck and pulled out another one.

"This is amazing!" I cried happily. "These will terrify those kids. How will I ever choose the best one?"

Chuck let out a disgusted groan and dropped the mask he was holding into the box. "They feel like real skin. They're so warm."

I didn't pay any attention to him. I was busy digging down to the bottom of the carton. I wanted to check out each mask before I made my choice.

I wanted the scariest, grossest mask in the box. I wanted a mask that would give those first graders more nightmares than they had given me!

I pulled out a mask of a girl's face with a lizard's head poking out from her mouth.

No. Not scary enough.

I pulled out a mask of a snarling wolf, its lips

40

pulled back to show two jagged rows of pointed teeth.

Too wimpy.

I pulled out an ugly mask of a leering old man, his mouth twisted in an evil grin. One long, crooked tooth stuck down over his lower lip.

The mask had long, stringy yellow hair that drooped down over the old man's craggy forehead. I could see big black spiders climbing in the hair and in the ears. A chunk of forehead was missing, revealing a patch of gray skull underneath.

Not bad, I thought.

This one even *smelled* bad!

I started to put it back when I heard a creaking sound again.

Louder this time.

The ceiling above my head groaned.

I gasped. It really sounded like a footstep. Someone walking around up there.

But the store had appeared dark and empty. Chuck and I had both stared into the window for a long time. If anyone was hiding there in the darkness, we would have seen them.

Another *creak* made me suck in a mouthful of air.

I froze, listening hard. I could hear the steady *drip drip* of water across the dark basement. I could hear the trapdoor rattling outside.

And I could hear my own shallow breathing.

The ceiling squeaked. I swallowed hard.

It's an old building, I told myself. All old build-
ings squeak and creak. Especially on a windy
night.

A scraping footstep made me gasp out loud.

"Chuck — did you hear that?"

Gripping the old-man mask, I listened hard.

"Did you hear that?" I whispered. "Do you think
someone else is in the building?"

Silence.

Another scraping footstep.

"Chuck?" I whispered. "Hey — Chuck?"

My heart pounding, I turned to him.

"Chuck?"

He was gone.

9

"Chuck?"

A stab of fear made my breath catch in my throat.

I heard the hard thud of sneakers against concrete, and turned to the stairs. In the dim light, I saw Chuck disappear out through the trapdoor.

As soon as he reached the alley, he poked his head back in. "Steve — get *out!*" he called down in a loud whisper. "Hurry! Get *out* of there!"

Too late.

A ceiling light flashed on.

As I blinked against the bright light, I saw a man move quickly across the basement. He swept along the wall, pulled a long, black cord — and the trapdoor slammed shut with a deafening *clang*.

"Oh!" I uttered a weak cry as he turned angrily to me.

I was trapped.

Chuck got out. But I was trapped. Trapped in the basement with this guy.

And what a weird-looking guy! To begin with, he wore a long black cape that swept behind him as he crossed the room to me.

Is that a Halloween costume? I wondered.

Does he wear a black cape all the time?

Beneath the billowing cape, he wore a black suit, kind of old-fashioned looking.

He had shiny black hair, parted in the middle and slicked down with some kind of hair grease, and a pencil-thin, black mustache that curled over his upper lip.

As he stood over me, his black eyes glowed like two burning coals.

Like vampire eyes! I thought.

My whole body was shaking. I gripped the sides of the carton and tried to return his stare.

Trapped, I thought, waiting for him to speak. Trapped with a vampire.

"What are you doing here?" he asked finally. He pushed back his cape and crossed his arms in front of him. The glowing eyes glared down at me sternly.

"Uh . . . just looking at masks," I managed to choke out. I was still on my knees on the floor. I knew that my legs were shaking too hard to stand up.

"The store is closed," the man said through gritted teeth.

44

"I know," I admitted, lowering my eyes to the floor. "I — "

"The store went out of business. We're closed for good."

"I . . . I'm sorry," I murmured.

Was he going to let me go? What was he going to do with me?

If I started to scream, no one would hear me.

Would Chuck try to get help for me? Or was he halfway home by now?

"I live upstairs," the man explained, still glaring at me angrily. "I heard scraping sounds down here. Boxes being moved around. I was going to call the police."

"I'm not a burglar," I blurted out. "Please don't call the police. The trapdoor was open and my friend and I came down."

His eyes moved quickly around the room. "Your friend?"

"He ran away when he heard you coming," I told him. "I just wanted to see if there were any masks. You know. For Halloween. I wasn't going to steal anything. I just — "

"But the store is closed," the man repeated. He glanced at the open carton in front of me. "Those masks are very special. They're not for sale."

"N-not for sale?" I stammered.

"You shouldn't break into stores," the man replied, shaking his head. His slicked-down hair gleamed under the low ceiling light. "How old are you?"

I drew a blank. My mouth dropped open, but no answer came out. I was so terrified, I forgot how old I was!

"Twelve," I answered finally. I took a deep breath, trying to calm myself.

"Twelve and you're already breaking into stores," the man said softly.

"I don't break into stores!" I protested. "I mean, I never did before. I came to buy a mask. Look. I brought money."

I jammed my trembling hand into my jeans pocket and pulled out the wad of bills. "Twenty-five dollars," I said, holding up the money so he could see it. "Here. Is it enough for one of these masks?"

He rubbed his chin. "I told you, young man. These masks are special. They cannot be sold. Believe me — you do not want one of these."

"But I do!" I cried. "They're awesome! They're the best masks I've ever seen. Halloween is only a few days away. I need one. I need one desperately. Please — !"

"No!" the man shouted sharply. "Not for sale."

"But why not?" I wailed.

He eyed me thoughtfully. "Too real," he replied. "The masks are too real."

"But that's why they're so awesome!" I ex-

claimed. "Please? *Please?* Take my money. Here."
I pushed the wad of bills toward him.

He didn't reply. Instead, he turned away. His
cape swirled behind him. "Come with me, young
man."

"Huh? Where?" Cold fear ran down my back. I
was still holding the money out in front of me.

"Come upstairs with me. I'm going to call your
parents."

"No!" I shrieked. "Please — !"

If my mom and dad found out I got caught
breaking into the basement of a store, they would
go totally ballistic! They'd ground me for life! I'd
miss this Halloween — and the next thirty Hal-
loweens to come!

The man eyed me coldly. "I don't want to call
the police," he said softly. "I'd rather call your
parents."

"Please . . ." I murmured again, climbing to my
feet.

I suddenly had an idea.

I could make a run for it.

I glanced quickly at the concrete stairs leading
up to the trapdoor. If I took off — and really
flew — I could get up those stairs before the man
could reach me.

The trapdoor was shut. But it probably wasn't
locked. I could push it open from underneath, and
just keep running.

I glanced again at the steps. It was worth a try, I decided.

I took a deep breath and held it.

Then I silently counted to three.

One . . . two . . . THREE!

On three, I took off. My heart thudded louder than my sneakers on the hard floor. But I made it to the stairs in about a second and a half!

"Hey — stop!" I heard the caped man cry out in surprise. I could hear his heavy steps as he plunged after me.

"Stop, young man! Where are you going?"

I didn't slow down or glance back.

I took the stairs two at a time.

Yes! Yes! I'm getting away! I thought.

As I reached the top, I shot out both hands — and pushed up on the trapdoor with all of my might.

It didn't budge.

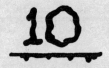

10

"Ohh!" I let out a terrified moan.

The caped man had reached the bottom of the steps. I could practically feel his breath on the back of my neck.

The door has *got* to open! I told myself. It's *got* to!

I took a deep breath. Then I heaved my shoulder against the door. I uttered a desperate groan as I pushed.

Pushed.

The caped man made a grab for me.

I felt his hand brush my ankle.

I kicked the hand away. Then I shoved my shoulder hard against the trapdoor.

And it opened.

"Yes!" A happy cry escaped my throat as I scrambled out into the alley.

The cold air rushed against my hot face. I stumbled over something hard — a stone or a brick. I didn't stop to look. I ran through the narrow alley, to the sidewalk in front of the store.

My eyes swept back and forth. I searched for Chuck. No sign of him.

Had the caped man followed me out the trap-door? Was he chasing after me?

I turned back to the alley. And saw only darkness.

Then I took off, running fast, my feet practically flying over the pavement. I shot across the street. Bright lights washed over me. A car horn honked, making me jump about a mile! The car roared past.

"Hey, Steve — !"

Chuck stepped out from behind a tall evergreen shrub. "You made it!"

"Yeah. I made it," I replied, gasping for breath.

"I — I didn't know what to do!" he stammered.

I shook my head. "So you just stood here?"

"I waited for you," he said. "I was kind of scared."

Big help.

"Get going," I urged, glancing back across the street. "He may be chasing us."

We ran side by side, our breath steaming up into the cold night air. The houses and dark lawns whirred past in a gray-black blur. We didn't say another word to each other.

Three blocks later, I slowed down as we reached

Chuck's house. I leaned over and tried to shake away the sharp pain in my side. I always get a pain like that when I run more than a few blocks.

"See you!" Chuck cried breathlessly. "Sorry you didn't get your mask."

"Yeah. It's too bad," I murmured glumly.

I watched him run along the side of his house until he disappeared around the back. Then I took a deep breath and took off again, jogging now, toward my house on the next block.

My heart was still racing in my chest. But I was starting to feel calmer. The man in the black cape didn't chase after us. In a few seconds, I would be safe in my own home.

Halfway up our driveway, I slowed to a stop. The pain in my side had faded to a dull ache.

I stepped into the yellow light from the front porch. I could hear my dog Sparky barking inside the house. Sparky knew I was home.

As I climbed onto the front stoop, a smile crossed my face.

A very wide smile.

I was pleased with myself. In fact, I was overjoyed. I felt like leaping in the air. Or maybe doing a wild, crazy dance. Or crowing like a rooster. Or tilting back my head and howling at the moon.

The evening had been a total success.

I didn't tell Chuck. I didn't want Chuck to know. But when the caped man clicked on the basement light — in that split second before he saw me and I saw him — I grabbed a mask from the carton. And I shoved it under my sweatshirt.

I had a mask!

It hadn't been easy. In fact, being trapped in that eerie basement with that strange man had been the scariest time of my life.

But I had a mask! Safely tucked under my sweatshirt.

I could feel it against my chest as I ran. And I could feel it now, warm against my skin as I reached for the front door.

I was so happy. So pleased with myself.

And then I felt the mask start to move.

And I screamed as something sharp bit into my chest.

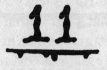

11

I grabbed the front of my sweatshirt. I pressed both hands tight against the bulge of the mask.

"Whoa," I murmured, holding the mask in place under the sweatshirt.

Stop imagining things, Steve, I scolded myself.

Calm down. The mask started to slip down your chest. That's all. It wasn't moving. It didn't bite you.

Get in the house, I ordered myself. Hide the thing in a drawer in your room. And pull yourself together.

Why was I so nervous?

The scary part was over. I had escaped with one of the great masks. Now it was my turn to scare *other* people. Why was I standing there scaring myself?

Still holding the front of my sweatshirt, I pushed open the front door and stepped into the house. "Down, boy! Get down, Sparky!" I cried as the little black terrier greeted me. He leaped high off the floor, bouncing off me, barking and whining as if he hadn't seen me in twenty years.

"Get down, Sparky! Down!"

I wanted to sneak into the house, run up to my room, and stash the mask away before my parents heard me return. But Sparky ruined that plan.

"Steve — is that you?" Mom stormed into the living room, a fretful frown on her face. She glared at me and angrily blew a curl of blond hair from in front of her eyes. "Where on earth were you? Your father and I went ahead and ate dinner. Yours is ice-cold by now!"

"Sorry, Mom," I said, still holding the front of my sweatshirt to keep the mask in place as I tried to push Sparky away.

The lock of hair fell back over her forehead. She blew at it again. "Well? Where *were* you?"

"I . . . well . . ."

Think fast, Steve.

You can't tell her you sneaked out to steal a Halloween mask from the basement of a store.

"I had to help Chuck with something," I finally answered.

Sure, it was a lie. But it wasn't a serious lie.

I'm usually a very honest guy. But right then, all I cared about was having the mask! I had it, and I was desperate to get it out from under my sweatshirt and hidden in a safe place in my room.

"Well, you should have told me where you were

54

going," Mom scolded. "Your father went out to do the grocery shopping. But he's very angry, too. You should have been home for dinner."

I lowered my head. "Sorry, Mom."

Sparky gazed up at me. Was he staring at the bulge in my sweatshirt?

If the dog could see it, Mom could see it too.

"I'll take off my coat and come right down," I told her.

I didn't give her a chance to reply. I spun around, leaped onto the stairs, and ran up two at a time. I flew down the hall, burst into my room, and slammed the door behind me.

I took a few seconds to catch my breath. I listened hard, making sure that Mom hadn't followed me upstairs.

No. I could hear her banging around in the kitchen, getting my dinner ready.

I couldn't *wait* to check out the mask!

Which one did I take? When the light came on in the store basement, I grabbed a mask without looking. I stuffed it under my sweatshirt before I could see it.

Now I eagerly reached under the sweatshirt and pulled out my hard-won prize.

"Wow!" I raised it in both hands and admired it.

The old-man mask. I took the mask of the creepy old man.

I smoothed out its long strings of yellow-white hair. Holding it by the big, pointy ears, I lifted it in front of my face and examined it closely.

A single white tooth hung down over the bottom lip. A brown wormhole poked through the center of the tooth.

Outside on the front stoop, the big tooth had scraped my chest, I realized. That's what made me think the mask was biting me.

The mouth was twisted in an evil sneer. The lips curled like two brown worms.

The long nose had gobs of green dripping from each nostril. A square patch of skin was missing just above the forehead. I could see gray skull bone in the hole.

The whole face was creased and lined. The flesh was a sickly green. The skin appeared to be peeling off the face. Dark scabs bulged from the sunken cheeks.

Black spiders appeared to crawl through the stringy, yellow hair. Spiders poked out of the two ears.

"Yuck!" I cried.

Was I holding the scariest Halloween mask in the world?

No. In the universe!

I began to feel a little queasy just holding it. I rubbed the scabby cheek with one finger. The skin felt warm, like real skin.

"Heh-heh-heh." I practiced laughing like an old man. "Heh-heh-heh." I tried a dry cackle.

Look out, Hogs! I told myself. When I come leaping out at you on Halloween night in this mask, you will jump out of your skins!

"Heh-heh-heh."

I raked the ugly, long hair back over the head. My fingers bumped over the spiders tangled in the hair. The spiders didn't feel rubbery. They felt soft and warm like the skin.

I gazed down happily at the disgusting, old face. It sneered back at me. The brown worm lips quivered.

Should I try it on?

I carried it over to the mirror on my closet door. I was dying to see what I'd look like.

I'll slip it on for just a second, I decided. Long enough to see how ugly and frightening I'd look.

Holding it in both hands, I raised the mask over my head.

Then slowly, carefully . . . very carefully . . . I began to pull the mask down, down, down over my face.

12

"*Steve — !*"

Mom's loud cry from downstairs startled me.

"Steve — where are you? Get down here for your dinner!"

"Coming!" I shouted back. I lowered the mask. I'd try it on later, I decided.

I walked quickly to the dresser and pulled open my sock drawer. Smoothing the long, spidery hair over the ugly face, I set the mask down carefully in the drawer. Then I hid it under several pairs of socks and closed the drawer.

I hurried down to the kitchen. Mom had a salad on the table and a plate of warmed-up macaroni-and-cheese.

My stomach growled. I suddenly realized that I was starved! I sat down, pushed the salad aside, and started forking up the macaroni as fast as I could.

I glanced down to see Sparky staring up at me

with his big, black, soulful eyes. He saw me looking at him and tilted his head.

"Sparky," I said, "you don't like macaroni — remember?"

He tilted his head the other way, as if trying to understand. I slipped him a couple of noodles. He sniffed them and left them on the floor.

Behind me, Mom busily cleaned out the refrigerator, making room for the groceries Dad was out buying. I was *dying* to tell her about the scary mask. I wanted to show it to her. Maybe put it on and make her scream.

But I knew she'd ask too many questions about where I bought it, and how much it cost, and how much of my allowance I used up to pay for it.

All questions I couldn't answer.

So I bit my tongue and forced myself not to blurt out the exciting news that I wouldn't have to be a hobo again this Halloween.

That was my costume for the past five years. A hobo. Actually, it wasn't much of a costume. I wore one of Dad's baggy old suits with patches on the pants. Mom rubbed charcoal on my face to make me look dirty. And I carried a knapsack on a fishing pole over my shoulder.

Bor-ring!

This Halloween will be different, I promised myself. This Halloween will not be boring.

I was so happy. As I sat gobbling down

macaroni-and-cheese, I couldn't get that creepy mask out of my mind.

I'm not going to tell *anyone* about it, I decided. I'm going to scare everyone I know.

I'm not even going to tell Chuck. After all, he ran away and left me down in that dark basement.

Look out, Chuckie Boy! I told myself, grinning so hard some noodles slipped out of my mouth. I'm going to get you too!

13

I had soccer practice for my first graders after school the next day. It was a sunny, cold October afternoon. The sunlight made the yellow and brown falling leaves glitter like gold. Puffs of white cloud floated like soft cotton across the blue sky.

Everything looked beautiful to me. Because Halloween was only one day away.

I was staring up at the clouds when Marnie Rosen drop-kicked the soccer ball into my stomach.

I grabbed my stomach and doubled over in pain. Duck Benton and two other kids jumped on my back and drove me facedown into the mud.

I didn't care.

In fact, I laughed.

Because I knew that I had only one day to wait.

I tried to show them how to pass. As I ran along the sidelines, Andrew Foster stuck out his foot. I tripped and went sailing into the bike rack. A handlebar caught me under the chin as I fell, and I actually saw stars.

But I didn't care.

I picked myself up with a grin on my face.

Because I knew a secret. I knew an evil secret that the kids didn't know. I knew that trick-or-treat night was going to be a *special* treat for me!

At four o'clock, I called an end to practice. I was too weak to blow the whistle. My clothes were soaked with mud, I walked with a limp, and I had cuts and bruises in twenty different places.

A typical practice with the Horrible Hogs.

But did I care?

You know the answer.

I gathered them in a circle around me. They were shoving each other, and pulling hair, and calling each other horrible names. I told you — they're total animals.

I raised my hands to quiet them down. "Let's have a special Hogs' Halloween party tomorrow," I suggested.

"YAAAY!" they cheered.

"We'll meet in our costumes after practice," I continued. "The whole team. And we'll all go trick-or-treating together. I'll take you."

"YAAY!" they cheered again.

"So tell your parents to drop you off," I told them. "This is going to be our special party. We'll meet in front of the old Carpenter mansion."

Silence. This time they didn't cheer.

"Why do we have to meet there?" Andrew asked.

"Isn't that old house supposed to be haunted?" Marnie asked softly.

"That place is too creepy," Duck added.

I narrowed my eyes at them, challenging them. "You guys aren't *scared* — are you?" I demanded.

Silence. They exchanged nervous glances.

"Well? Are you all too wimpy to meet me there?" I asked.

"No way!" Marnie insisted.

"No way! We're not scared of a stupid old house!"

They all began to tell me how brave they were. They all said they would meet me there.

"I saw a ghost once," Johnny Myers bragged. "Behind my garage. I shouted 'Boo!' and it floated away."

These kids are animals, but they have great imaginations.

The other kids all started teasing Johnny. He stuck to his story. He insisted he saw a ghost. So they pushed him to the ground and got his jacket all muddy.

"Hey, Steve — what are you going to be for Halloween?" Marnie asked.

"Yeah. What's your costume?" Andrew demanded.

"He's going to be a pile of toxic waste!" someone joked.

"No. He's going to be a ballerina!" someone else declared.

They all hooted and jeered.

Go ahead and laugh, guys, I thought. Have a good laugh now. Because when you see me on Halloween, I'll be the only one laughing.

"Uh . . . I'm going to be a hobo," I told them. "You'll recognize me. I'll be wearing a tattered old suit. And my face will be all dirty. I'll be dressed like a bum."

"You *are* a bum!" one of my loyal team members shouted.

More wild laughing and hooting. More shoving and hair-pulling and wrestling on the ground.

Luckily, their parents and baby-sitters showed up to take them home. I watched them go with a big smile on my face. A big, evil smile.

Then I grabbed up my backpack and hurried home. I ran all the way. I was eager to take another look at my mask.

Chuck stepped out as I jogged past his house. "Hey, Steve . . . what's up?" he called.

"Not much!" I called back. "Later, man!"

I kept running. I didn't want to hang out with Chuck. I needed to check out that mask. I needed to remind myself of how awesome it was. How totally terrifying.

I burst through the front door. Then I ran straight up the stairs to my room, taking the stairs three at a time.

I raced down the long hall. I turned into my room and tossed my backpack onto the bed. Then I hurried across the room to my dresser and eagerly jerked open my sock drawer.

"Huh?"

I peered inside. With a trembling hand, I shoved away several balled-up pairs of socks.

The mask was gone.

14

"No!"

I began pawing frantically through the drawer, tossing all the socks onto the floor.

No mask. Gone.

The balled-up socks bounced all over the room. My heart was bouncing too.

Then I remembered that I had moved the mask. Before school that morning. I was worried that my mom might do laundry. And open my sock drawer. And see it there.

So I had shoved it to the back of my closet, behind my rolled-up sleeping bag.

Letting out a long whoosh of air, I dropped to my hands and knees. I quickly collected all the socks and stuffed them back into the drawer. Then I opened the closet door and pulled down the mask from the top shelf.

Steve, you've got to calm down, man, I told myself. It's just a Halloween mask, after all. You've got to stop scaring yourself like that.

Sometimes it helps to scold yourself, to give yourself advice.

I started to feel a little calmer. I smoothed back the stringy yellow hair and rubbed my hand over the craggy, scab-covered skin of the mask.

The brown lips sneered at me. I poked my little finger through the disgusting wormhole in the tooth. I squeezed the spiders hiding inside the ears.

"This is *so cool!*" I declared out loud.

I couldn't wait a whole day till Halloween. I had to show it to someone.

No. I had to *scare* someone with it.

Chuck's face popped instantly into my mind. My old friend Chuck was the perfect victim. I knew that he was home. I had seen him there a few minutes ago.

Wow. Will he be shocked! I told myself. Chuck thought that I ran out of that store basement empty-handed. When I sneak into his house and creep up on him wearing this disgusting mask, he'll *faint!*

I glanced at the clock. I had an hour before dinnertime. Mom and Dad weren't even home yet.

Yes, I'll do it! I decided.

"Heh-heh-heh." I practiced my old-man cackle. "Heh-heh-heh." The scariest, most evil cackle I could do.

Then I grasped the wrinkled neck of the mask

67

in both hands. Stepping in front of the mirror, I raised the mask over my head.

And tugged it down.

It slid easily over my hair. It felt soft and warm as I pulled it over my face.

Down over my ears. Over my cheeks.

Down, down.

Until I felt the top of the mask settle onto my hair. I twisted it until I could see out of the narrow eyeholes.

Then I lowered my hands to my sides and stepped closer to the mirror to check myself out.

So warm.

I suddenly felt too warm.

The rubbery mask pressed tightly against my cheeks and forehead.

Warmer.

"Hey — !" I cried out as my face began to burn.

So hot . . .

So hard to breathe.

"Hey . . . what is *happening* to me?"

15

I could feel the skin of the mask tightening around my face.

My cheeks burned. A sour odor swept over me, choked me.

I gagged. I sucked in a deep breath through my mouth. But the mask was so tight, I could hardly breathe.

I grabbed the ears with both hands. The outside of the mask felt normal. But inside, I was burning up!

I tried to tug the mask off. But it wouldn't slide up. The hot rubber stuck to my face.

I groaned as the putrid odor washed over me again.

I tugged harder. The mask didn't budge.

I gasped for breath.

I grabbed the stringy hair — and pulled. I slid my hands under the chin — and pushed.

"Ohhh." A sick groan escaped my throat. My hands dropped limply to my sides.

I suddenly felt so tired. So weak.

So totally weak.

Every breath was a struggle. I bent over. My body began to tremble.

I felt so weak. And old.

Old.

Was this how an old man felt?

Calm down, Steve, I scolded myself. It's just a rubber mask. It fits a little too snug, that's all.

It's stuck to your face. But you'll pull it off, and you'll be fine.

Calm down. Count to ten. Then examine the mask in the mirror. Grab it from the bottom, and you'll be able to pull it up. No problem.

I counted to ten. Then I stepped up close to the mirror.

I nearly cried out when I saw my reflection. The mask really was awesome! So real. So gross.

With my eyes staring out of it, the face seemed to come alive. The brown lips sneered back at me. When I moved *my* lips, they appeared to move too. The green gobs of goo trembled inside the big nostrils. The spiders appeared to be crawling through the tangled, yellow hair.

It's only a mask. A really cool mask, I said to myself.

I started to feel a little calmer.

But then a cackle escaped my throat. "Heh-heh-heh."

Not my cackle!

Not in my voice! An old man's cackle.

How did that happen? How did I utter such a strange sound?

I clamped my lips shut. I didn't want to make that sound again.

"Heh-heh-heh."

Another frightening cackle! In a shrill, high-pitched voice. More like a dry croak than a laugh.

I tightened my jaw. Clenched my teeth. Held my breath so I wouldn't cackle again.

"Heh-heh-heh."

I wasn't doing it!

Who was cackling like that?

Where was the shrill, dry laugh coming from?

I gaped at the old face in the mirror, suddenly frozen in fear.

And then I felt a strong hand grab my leg.

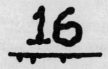

16

With a choked gasp, I whirled around.

And peered down through the tight eyeholes of the mask.

I instantly saw that it wasn't a hand on my leg. It was teeth.

Dog teeth.

"Sparky — it's you!" I cried. But my voice came out in a dry whisper.

Sparky backed away.

I cleared my throat and tried again. "Don't be afraid, Sparky. It's only me." My voice! It sounded more like a dry cough.

It sounded like my grandpa!

I had an old man's face — and an old man's voice.

And I felt so tired. So totally weak and tired.

As I reached to pet Sparky, my arms drooped as if they weighed a thousand pounds. Both of my knees cracked as I bent down.

The dog gazed up at me and tilted his head. His short stub of a tail wagged furiously.

"Don't be scared, Sparky," I croaked. "I was just trying out this mask. Pretty scary, huh?"

I lowered my face and tried to pick Sparky up.

But as I leaned forward, I could see the dog's eyes go wide with terror. Sparky let out a shrill *yip* — jumped out of my hands, and went tearing across the room, barking at the top of his lungs. Barking in total fright.

"Sparky — it's me!" I cried. "I know I sound different. But it's me — Steve!"

I wanted to chase after him. But my legs felt so weak, and my knees refused to bend.

It took me three tries to pull myself up to a standing position. My head ached. I was too out-of-breath to run after Sparky.

Too late, anyway. I could hear him barking his head off, already downstairs.

"Weird," I muttered, rubbing my aching back. I hobbled back to the mirror. Sparky has seen masks before. He knew it was me. Why was he so scared? Was it my weird voice?

How had the mask dried up my voice? And why did I suddenly feel one hundred and ten?

At least, my face no longer felt on fire. But the skin of the mask still pressed so tightly against my face, I could barely move my lips.

I have to get out of this thing, I decided. Chuck

will have to wait until Halloween night to be scared out of his skull.

I raised both hands to my neck and searched for the bottom of the mask. My neck felt craggy and wrinkled. The skin was dry.

Where was the bottom of the mask?

I leaned close to the mirror on my closet door and narrowed my eyes at my reflection. I stared hard at the neck of the mask.

Wrinkled skin flecked with ugly brown patches.

But where was the bottom? Where did the mask end and my neck begin?

My hands began to tremble as they fumbled up and down my throat. I could feel my heart begin to race.

I moved my hands slowly, carefully, up and down my neck.

Again. And again.

Finally, I let my hands drop to my side and uttered a weary, frightened sigh.

There *was* no mask bottom. No line at all between the mask and my neck.

The wrinkled, spotted mask skin had become *my* skin.

"Nooooo! Nooooo!" I wailed in my old man's voice. I had to get the thing off me! There had to be a way!

I squeezed the cheeks of the mask and tugged with all my might.

"Ow!" Sharp pain ran down my face.

I pulled the hair. That sent a wave of pain shooting down my scalp. Frantically, I grabbed at the mask, slapped at it, pulled it, tore at it.

I felt each move. Each slap and tug made my skin hurt. Every touch hurt me as if it were my own skin.

"The eyeholes!" I croaked.

I reached for the eyeholes. Maybe I could slip my fingers inside the eyeholes and lift the mask off.

My hands fumbled around my eyes. My trembling fingers searched, poking and rubbing.

No eyeholes. There were no eyeholes.

The rutted, scab-covered skin had melted onto me. It had become *my* skin.

The ugly, disgusting mask had become *my* face!

I looked like a horrifying, spider-infested, decaying old man. And I felt as old and weird as I looked!

My throat tightened in terror. I sank against the mirror, pressing my ugly, craggy forehead against the glass.

I shut my eyes. What can I do? What can I do? The question repeated like an unhappy chant in my mind.

And then I heard the front door slam. And I heard Mom's voice at the bottom of the stairway. "Steve — are you home? Steve?"

What can I do? What can I do? The question repeated and repeated.

"Steve?" Mom called. "Come down here. I want to show you something."

No! I thought, swallowing hard, my dry throat making a sick clicking sound. *No! I can't come down! I can't! I don't want you to see me like this!*

"Oh, never mind!" Mom called. "I'm coming up there!"

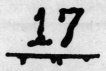

17

I heard her footsteps on the stairs.

A shock of panic made me lurch toward the door. I nearly fell over. My old legs were stiff, too stiff to move quickly.

I hobbled to the door and closed it just as Mom reached the second floor. Then I leaned against the door, my hand on my throbbing chest, trying to catch my breath.

Trying to think. Trying to decide what to say.

I couldn't let her see me like this. I couldn't let her see the mask. She'd start asking questions. And I couldn't let her see how the mask had changed me.

A few seconds later, she knocked gently on the door. "Steve, are you in there? What are you doing?"

"Uh . . . nothing, Mom."

"Well, may I come in? I brought you something."

"Not right now," I croaked.

Please don't open the door! I begged silently. *Please don't come into my room!*

"Steve, why do you sound so strange?" Mom demanded. "What's wrong with your voice?"

"Uh . . ." *Think fast, Steve. Think fast.*

"Uh . . . sore throat, Mom. A really bad sore throat."

"Let me take a look at you. Are you sick?" Glancing down, I saw the doorknob turn.

"No!" I screamed, pressing my back against the door.

"You're not sick?"

"I mean, yes," I croaked in my shaky, old-man voice. "I'm not feeling well, Mom. I'm going to lie down for a while. I'll come down later, okay?"

I stared at the doorknob, listening to her breathing on the other side of the door. "Steve, I bought you those black-and-white cookies that you love. Your favorites. Do you want one? Maybe it'll make you feel better."

My stomach growled. Those cookies are my favorites. Dripping with chocolate icing on one side and vanilla icing on the other. "Maybe later," I moaned.

"But I drove two miles out of my way to buy them for you," Mom said.

"Later. I'm really not feeling well." I was telling the truth. My temples throbbed. My whole body ached. I felt so weak, I could barely stand up.

"I'll call you for dinner," Mom said. I listened to her make her way back down the stairs. Then I hobbled over to the bed and slumped my old man's body down onto the edge.

"Now what?" I asked myself. I pressed my hands against my scabby cheeks. "How do I get out of this thing?"

I shut my tired, burning eyes and tried to think. After a few minutes, Carly Beth's face floated into my mind.

"Yes!" I croaked. "Carly Beth is the one person in the world who can help me."

Carly Beth wore a mask from the same store last Halloween. Maybe the same thing happened to her. Maybe her mask stuck to her face and changed her.

She got her mask off. She will know how I can get my mask off too.

The phone stood across the room beside the computer on my desk. Normally, I'd be over there in three seconds. But it took me three minutes of grunting and straining to get my old body to stand up. Then it took another five minutes to drag myself across the room.

By the time I dropped into my desk chair, I was exhausted. It took all of my strength to raise my hand and punch in Carly Beth's number on the phone.

I can't go on like this, I told myself. She's got to help me. She's *got* to know how to get this mask off.

After the third ring, Carly Beth's father answered. "Hello?"

"Hi . . . uh . . . could I speak to Carly Beth?" I choked out.

A silence. Then: "Who is this?" Mr. Caldwell sounded confused.

"It's me," I answered. "Is Carly Beth there?"

"Is this one of her teachers?" he demanded.

"No. It's Steve. I — "

"I'm sorry, sir. I can't hear you very well. Can you speak up? Why did you wish to speak to my daughter? Perhaps I can help you?"

"No . . . I — "

I heard Mr. Caldwell speak softly to someone else at his house. "It's an old man, asking for Carly Beth. I can barely hear him. He won't say who he is."

He came back on the phone. "Are you one of her teachers, sir? Where do you know my daughter from?"

"She's my friend," I croaked.

I heard him turn again to someone else in the room, probably Carly Beth's mom. He muffled the phone with his hand, but I heard what he said: "I think it's a nut. Some kind of crank call."

He returned to me. "Sorry, sir. My daughter can't come to the phone." He hung up.

I sat there listening to the buzz in my spider-filled ear.

Now what? I asked myself.

Now what?

18

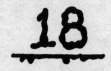

I must have fallen asleep in the desk chair. I don't know how long I slept.

I was awakened by Dad pounding on my bedroom door. "Steve — dinnertime!" he called in.

I sat up with a start. My back ached from sleeping sitting up. I rubbed my wrinkled neck, trying to rub away the stiffness.

"Steve — are you coming down to dinner?" Dad asked.

"I — I'm not very hungry," I croaked. "I'm going to take a nap, Dad. I think I'm getting sick."

"Hey, don't get sick the night before Halloween," he replied. "You don't want to miss out on trick-or-treating."

"I — I'll be okay," I stammered in my hoarse voice. "If I get a good night's sleep, I'll be fine."

Yeah. Right.

I'll be one hundred and fifty. But I'll be fine.

I let out an unhappy sigh.

"We'll bring you up some soup or something

later," Dad called in. Then he disappeared down-stairs.

I stared at the phone. Should I try Carly Beth again?

No, I decided. She won't believe it's me. She'll hang up the way her father did.

I scratched my ears. I could feel the spiders crackling around in them. I touched the bare spot on top of my head where the skin was ripped apart. The skin was soft and wet. I could feel the patch of hard skull that showed through.

"Ohhhh." Another long sigh.

I've got to think, I told myself. I've got to think of a way out of this.

But I felt so weary, so sleepy.

I pulled myself up and slumped to the bed. A few seconds later, I fell sound asleep.

I awoke to bright sunlight streaming through my bedroom window.

I blinked several times, startled by the bright morning light. Morning. Halloween morning.

It should have been a happy day. An exciting day. But instead . . .

I reached up with both hands and touched the sides of my face.

Smooth!

My cheeks felt smooth. Soft and smooth.

I rubbed my ears. Small ears. *My* ears. No spiders!

I raised both hands to my hair. And touched *my* hair. Not the stringy, old man's hair.

Hesitantly, carefully, I touched the torn spot on top of my head where the skull showed through.

Not there!

"I'm me again!" I cried out loud. I let out a long *whoop* of joy.

No old man's mask. No old man's voice. No old man's body.

It had all been a dream. A horrible nightmare.

Still blinking in the light, I gazed happily around my room.

"I dreamed it all!" I cried.

Going down to that dark store basement. Pawing through the carton of masks. The man in the cape. The mask of the old man. Sneaking it home and trying it on.

The mask sticking to my skin. Refusing to come off.

All a dream!

All a horrifying nightmare that was over now.

I was so happy! This had to be the happiest moment of my life.

I started to jump out of bed. I wanted to leap around my room, to dance for joy.

But then my eyes blinked open. And I woke up for real . . .

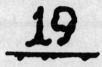

19

. . . I woke up for real.

And knew that I had only *dreamed* that it was all a dream!

I grabbed my face — and felt the craggy wrinkles, the heavy scabs. I rubbed my nose and brushed the green gobs stuck in my nostrils.

I had dreamed that the mask didn't exist.

I had dreamed that I had my own face back. My own voice and body.

All a dream. A wonderful dream.

But now I was really awake — and really in trouble.

I pulled myself up and brushed the stringy, yellow hair out of my eyes. "I have to tell Mom and Dad," I decided. "I can't spend another day like this."

I had slept in my clothes. I staggered to my feet and dragged my old body to the door. I tugged open the door — and saw a note taped on the other side.

Dear Steve,
Hope you're feeling better. Mom and I
had to go visit your Aunt Helen this
morning. We left early to beat the
traffic. We'll be home in time to help
you with your hobo costume. Love,
Dad

My hobo costume?

Not this year. Besides, since I was now at least one hundred and fifty, I was a little old to go trick-or-treating!

Crinkling the note in my hand, I made the long trip down to the kitchen, holding on to the banister, taking one step at a time. I had a sudden craving for a steaming bowl of oatmeal and a cup of hot milk.

"Oh, no!" I croaked. I was starting to *think* like an old man!

I made myself a breakfast of orange juice and corn flakes. I carried it to the table and sat down to eat. The juice glass felt strange against my fat, brown lips. And it was almost impossible to chew the cornflakes with just one long, crooked tooth.

"What am I going to do?" I moaned out loud.

Then, suddenly, I had an answer.

I decided to go ahead with my plan to terrify the first graders. Why shouldn't I pay back those bratty kids for all the trouble they gave me day after day on the soccer field?

Yes! I decided. When Mom and Dad get home, I'll greet them and show off my old-man costume. They won't know it isn't a costume. They'll think it's really cool.

Then, later, I'll go to the spooky old Carpenter mansion to meet the kids. And I'll scare the first graders out of their masks!

And then what?

Then I'll find Carly Beth. It won't be hard to find her. She's having a Halloween party at her house after trick-or-treating.

I'll find Carly Beth and get her to tell me the secret. I'll get her to show me how to remove this horrible mask.

Then I will be a very happy guy.

Sitting there alone in the kitchen, struggling to choke down my cornflakes, it seemed like a really good plan.

Too bad it didn't work out the way I hoped.

20

When Mom and Dad returned home that evening, I hobbled downstairs to greet them. They both gasped when they saw my ugly, scabby face.

Mom dropped the bag she was carrying. Her mouth fell open to her knees.

Dad's eyes bulged. He stared at me for a long time. Then he burst out laughing. "Steve — that is the *best* costume!" he exclaimed. "Where did you get that?"

"It's disgusting," Mom said. "Ohh. I can't stand that open patch on top of the head. And that horrible hole in your tooth."

Dad walked in a circle around me, admiring my new look.

I had put on the patched, black suit that I wore as my hobo costume. And I had found one of my grandpa's old canes in the closet, which I leaned on now.

"It's great!" Dad declared, squeezing my shoulder.

"I bought the mask at a party store," I croaked. It was *almost* the truth.

Mom and Dad exchanged glances. "The old man's voice is very good," Mom said. "Have you been practicing?"

"Yes. All day," I replied.

"Do you feel better?" Dad asked. "We didn't want to disturb you this morning since you weren't feeling good. Your mom and I had to leave so early . . ."

"I'm feeling much better," I lied. Actually, my legs were trembling and my whole body was drenched in a cold sweat.

Feeling weak, I leaned harder on the cane.

"Yuck! What's that in your hair?" Mom cried.

"Spiders," I told her. I shuddered. I could feel them crawling over my head and in my ears.

"They're so real-looking," Mom declared, raising a hand to her cheek. She shook her head. "Are you sure you don't want to be a hobo? That mask must be so hot and uncomfortable."

If she only knew how uncomfortable it was!

"Leave him be," Dad scolded her. "He looks great. He's going to terrify everyone on the street tonight."

I hope so, I thought. I glanced at my watch. Time to get going.

"Well, he's terrifying *me*!" Mom exclaimed. She shut her eyes. "I can't stand to look at you, Steve. Why did you buy something so . . . so ugly?"

"I think it's funny," Dad told her. He poked a finger at my long tooth. "Great mask. Is it rubber?"

"Yeah. I guess," I muttered in my quivering, old voice.

Mom made a disgusted face. "Are you trick-or-treating with Chuck?"

I yawned. I suddenly felt sleepy. "I promised my soccer players I'd meet them," I croaked. "Then I'm going over to Carly Beth's house."

"Well, don't stay out too late," Mom said. "And if that heavy mask gets too hot, take it off for a while — okay?"

I wish! I thought bitterly.

"See you later," I said. Leaning on the cane, I began dragging myself to the front door.

Mom and Dad laughed at my funny walk.

I wasn't laughing. I wanted to cry.

Only one thing kept me from breaking down and telling them the truth. Only one thing kept me from telling Mom and Dad that I was trapped inside this horrible mask, that it had turned me into a weak, ancient creature.

Revenge.

I could see the terrified expressions on the faces of my soccer team. And I could hear their howls of horror as they went running for their lives.

That cheered me up and kept me going.

I grabbed the doorknob and struggled to pull open the front door.

"Steve — wait!" Dad cried. "My camera. Wait. I want to take a picture." He disappeared in search of the camera.

"Your trick-or-treat bag!" Mom cried. "You forgot your trick-or-treat bag." She rummaged around in the front closet until she found the shopping bag with little pumpkins all over both sides.

I knew I couldn't manage the cane and the shopping bag. But I took it from her anyway. I'll throw the bag away when I get outside, I decided. I didn't plan to trick-or-treat. I knew it would take me half an hour just to walk up someone's driveway!

Dad burst back into the living room. "Say cheese!" he cried, raising his little camera.

I tried to twist my wormy lips into a smile.

Dad flashed the camera once. Then three more times.

Blinded by flashbulb lights, I said good-bye and made my way out the door. The white circles followed me into the night. I nearly fell off the front stoop.

I grabbed the railing and waited for my heart to stop pounding. Slowly the flashes of light faded from my eyes, and I began to pull myself down the driveway.

It was a clear, cold night. No wind at all. The nearly bare trees stood as still as statues.

I limped onto the sidewalk and started in the direction of the Carpenter mansion. There was no moon. But the street appeared brighter than usual. Most houses had all of their front lights on to welcome trick-or-treaters.

I stuffed the shopping bag into a trash can at the foot of our neighbors' driveway. Then I continued down the block, my cane tap-tapping on the sidewalk.

My back began to ache. My old legs trembled. I leaned over the cane, breathing hard.

After half a block, I had to take a rest against a lamppost. Luckily, the Carpenter mansion was on the next block.

As I started on my way, two little girls came hurrying down the sidewalk, followed by their father. One girl wore colorful butterfly wings. The other wore lots of makeup, a gold crown, and a long fancy dress.

"Ooh, he's ugly," the butterfly whispered to her friend as they came near.

"Yuck!" I heard the princess reply. "Look at the green stuff in his nose."

I leaned close to them, opened my lips in a snarl, and rasped, *Get out of my way!*

The little girls both let out frightened squeals and took off down the sidewalk. Their father flashed me an angry stare and hurried after them.

"Heh-heh-heh." An evil cackle escaped my lips.

Seeing their frightened faces gave me new energy. Leaning on my cane, I tap-tapped my way across the street.

A few minutes later, the Carpenter mansion came into view. The huge old house stood dark and empty. Its stone turrets rose up to the purple night sky like castle towers.

Huddled under a streetlamp at the bottom of the weed-choked front yard stood my soccer team. *My Hogs. My first graders.*

My victims.

They were all in costumes. I saw Power Rangers and Ninja Turtles. Mummies and monsters. Two ghosts, a Beauty, and a Beast.

But I recognized them anyway. I recognized them because they were shoving each other, grabbing at trick-or-treat bags, shouting and fighting.

I leaned against my cane, watching them from halfway down the block. My heart started to pound. My whole body trembled.

This was it. My big moment.

"Okay, guys," I murmured softly to myself. "It's *show time!*"

21

I was trembling with excitement as I dragged myself up to them. I stepped into the light, my wormy lips twisted in a frightening sneer.

I stared from one to another, giving them a chance to see my terrifying face. Giving them a chance to see the spiders crawling through my hair. The wormhole in my tooth. The patch of skull poking up through my rutted scalp.

They grew quiet. I could feel their eyes on me. I could sense their instant fear.

I opened my mouth to let out a frightening growl that would send them running for their mommies.

But Marnie Rosen, wearing a white bride's dress and veil, stepped up to me before I could get it out. "Can we help you, sir?" she asked.

"Are you lost?" one of the Power Rangers asked. "Do you need directions?"

"Can we help you get somewhere?"

No. No!

This wasn't going right. This wasn't going the way I'd planned — the way I'd dreamed!

Marnie took my arm. "Which way were you headed, sir? We'll walk with you. It's kind of a scary night to be walking around a strange neighborhood."

The others pushed in closer, trying to be helpful.

Trying to be helpful to an old man. An old man they weren't the least bit scared of.

"Nooooo!" I howled in protest. "I'm the ghost of the Carpenter mansion! I've come to pay you back for trespassing on my front yard!"

I tried to shriek — but my voice came out in a weak whisper. I don't think they heard a word I uttered.

I've got to scare them, I told myself. I've *got* to!

I raised both hands together in the air as if I planned to strangle them all.

My cane flew out of my grasp. I lost my balance and tottered over backward.

"Ohhhh!" I let out a groan as I hit the sidewalk sitting up.

They all cried out. But not in fear. They cried out because they were worried about me.

Helping hands reached down to pull me to my feet.

"Are you okay? Here's your cane." I recognized Duck Benton's scratchy voice.

I heard murmurs of sympathy. "Poor old guy," someone whispered.

"Are you hurt?"

"Can we get you some help?"

No. No. No. No. No.

They weren't terrified. The weren't the tiniest bit afraid.

I sank onto the cane. I suddenly felt so weary. So totally exhausted I could barely keep my head up.

Forget about scaring them, Steve, I told myself. You've got to get to Carly Beth's house before you collapse. You've got to find out from Carly Beth how to get the mask off. How to get your old face — and strength — back.

Marnie was still holding on to my trembling arm. "Where are you trying to go?" she asked, her freckled face filled with concern.

"Uh . . . do you know where Carly Beth Caldwell's house is?" I asked in a weak croak.

"It's on the next block. Across the street. I know her brother," I heard Andrew Foster say.

"We'll take you there," Marnie offered.

She gripped my arm tighter. A mummy stepped up and took my other arm. They began to walk me slowly, gently down the sidewalk.

I don't believe this! I thought bitterly. They're

supposed to be scared out of their costumes! They should be shrieking and crying by now.

But instead, they're *helping* me walk.

I sighed. The sad thing was, I felt so tired and weak, I couldn't have made it to Carly Beth's without their help.

They led me halfway up her driveway. Then I thanked them and told them I could make it the rest of the way.

I watched them scurry away to go trick-or-treating. "I guess Steve isn't going to show up," Duck said.

"He was probably too big a wimp to go out on Halloween night!" Marnie joked.

They all laughed.

Leaning heavily on the cane, I turned toward Carly Beth's house. The lights were all on. But I couldn't see anyone in the windows.

She probably isn't back from trick-or-treating yet, I decided.

I heard chattering voices. Footsteps on the gravel drive.

I wheeled around to see Carly Beth and her friend Sabrina Mason hurrying across the lawn, heading toward the house.

I recognized Carly Beth's duck costume. She wore it every year. Except for last Halloween, when she wore that terrifying mask.

Sabrina was some kind of superhero. She wore

silvery tights and a long silvery cape. She had a silvery mask pulled over her face, but I recognized her long, black hair.

"Carly Beth — !" I tried to shout. But her name came out in a choked whisper.

She and Sabrina kept chattering excitedly as they hurried across the lawn.

"Carly Beth — ! Please!" I cried.

Halfway to the house, they both turned. They saw me.

Yes!

"Carly Beth — " I cried.

She pulled off her duck mask and took a few steps toward the driveway. She squinted hard at me. "Who are you?"

"It's *me*!" I cried weakly. "I — "

"Are you the man who tried to call me earlier?" she demanded coldly.

"Well . . . yes," I croaked. "You see, I need — "

"Well, leave me alone!" Carly Beth screamed. "Why are you following me? Leave me alone, or I'll get my father!"

"But — but — but — " I sputtered helplessly.

The two girls spun away and began jogging to the house.

Leaving me standing there in the driveway.

Leaving me all alone.

Leaving me *doomed*.

22

I let out a bitter wail. "Carly Beth — it's me! It's me! Steve!" I cried. "Steve Boswell!"

Did she hear me?

Yes.

She and Sabrina had stepped onto the stone walk that led to the front porch. In the square of yellow light from the porch, I saw them both turn around.

"It's Steve! It's Steve!" I repeated, my throat aching from my desperate cries.

Slowly, cautiously, both girls made their way back to me.

"Steve?" Carly Beth stared hard at me, her mouth falling open.

"Is that a mask?" Sabrina demanded, keeping close to Carly Beth.

"Yes, it's a mask," I croaked.

"Yuck. It's disgusting!" Sabrina declared. She pulled off her silver mask to see better. "Are those spiders? Yuck!"

"I need help," I confessed. "This mask — "

"You went to the party store!" Carly Beth cried. The duck mask fell to the ground. She raised both hands to the sides of her face. "Oh, no! No! Steve, I warned you!"

"Yes. That's where I got it," I said, pointing to my hideous face. "I didn't listen to you. I didn't know."

"Steve, I told you not to go there," Carly Beth said, her expression still tight with horror. Hands still pressed against her cheeks.

"Now the mask won't come off," I wailed. "It's stuck to me. It's part of me. And it's — it's turning me into an old, old man. A feeble old man."

Carly Beth shook her head sadly. She stared at my ugly face, but didn't say a word.

"You've got to help me," I pleaded. "You've got to help me get this mask off."

Carly Beth let out a frightened sigh. "Steve — I don't think I can."

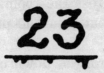

23

I grabbed her duck feathers and held on. "You've got to help me, Carly Beth," I begged. "Why won't you help me?"

"I *want* to help you," she explained. "But I'm not sure I can."

"But you had a mask from the same store last Halloween," I protested. "You pulled the mask off. You escaped from it — right?"

"It can't be pulled off," Carly Beth said. "There's no way to pull it off."

Over her shoulder, I saw three kids in costumes at the next house. A woman appeared in the doorway. I saw her dropping candy bars into the three trick-or-treat bags.

Some kids are having fun tonight, I thought bitterly.

I am *not* having fun tonight.

I may never have fun again.

"Come into the house," Carly Beth suggested. "It's cold out here. I'll try to explain."

I tried to follow them up the driveway. But my legs wobbled like rubber. Carly Beth and Sabrina practically had to carry me into her house. They dropped me down on the green leather couch in the living room.

On a table across the room, a carved jack-o'-lantern grinned at me. The pumpkin had more teeth than I did!

Carly Beth dropped down on the couch arm. Sabrina sat on the edge of the armchair beside it. She leaned over and sifted through her trick-or-treat bag. How could she think of candy at a time like this?

I turned to Carly Beth. "How do I get the mask off?" I croaked.

Carly Beth chewed her bottom lip. She raised her eyes to me, her expression grim. "It isn't a mask," she said softly.

"Excuse me?" I cried.

"It isn't a mask," she explained. "It's a real face. A living face. Did you meet the man in the black cape?"

I nodded.

"He's some kind of weird scientist, I think. He made the faces. In his lab."

"He — he *made* them?" I stammered.

Carly Beth nodded solemnly. "They are real, living faces. The man in the cape tried to make them good-looking. But something went wrong.

They all came out ugly. As ugly as the one you're wearing."

"But, Carly Beth — " I started.

She raised a hand to hush me. "The caped man calls the faces The Unloved. No one wants them because they turned out so ugly. They are The Unloved. They're alive. And they attach themselves to anyone who comes near enough."

"But how do I get it off?" I cried impatiently. I raised my hands and tugged at my rutted, scabby cheeks. "I can't spend the rest of my life like this. What can I do?"

Carly Beth jumped up and began pacing back and forth in front of Sabrina and me. Sabrina unwrapped a Milky Way bar and began chewing it, watching Carly Beth pace.

"The same thing happened to me last Halloween," Carly Beth said. "I had chosen a really ugly mask. It was so scary. It attached itself to my head. And then it turned me evil."

"And what did you do?" I cried, leaning forward on my cane.

"I went back to the party store. I found the man in the cape. He told me there was only one way to get rid of the mask. It could only be done with a symbol of love."

"Huh?" I gaped at her. I didn't understand.

"I had to find a symbol of love," Carly Beth continued. "At first, I didn't know what the man meant. I didn't know what to do. But then I remembered something my mom had made for me."

"What?" I demanded eagerly. "What was it?"

"It was that head," Sabrina chimed in, her mouth bulging with chocolate.

"My mom had sculpted a head of me," Carly Beth said. "It looked just like me. You've seen it. Mom sculpted it because she loves me. It was a symbol of love."

Carly Beth dropped back down beside me. "I placed Mom's sculpted head over The Unloved face. And The Unloved disappeared. The ugly face slipped right off."

"Great!" I cried happily. "Go get it. Hurry!"

"Huh?" Carly Beth stared at me, confused.

"Go get the sculpted head," I begged. "I've got to get this thing off me!"

Carly Beth shook her head. "You don't get it, Steve. You can't use *my* symbol of love. It will only work for me. You have to find *your own* symbol of love."

"But maybe it won't work for Steve's mask," Sabrina interrupted. "Maybe each mask is different."

"Give me a break, Sabrina," I muttered angrily. "It's got to work! Don't you understand? It's *got* to!"

"You have to find your own symbol of love," Carly Beth repeated. "Can you think of one, Steve?"

I stared back at her, thinking hard.

I thought. And thought.

Symbol of love . . . symbol of love . . .

No. I couldn't think of anything. Not a single thing.

And then an idea popped into my mind.

24

I leaned on the cane and tried to pull myself up from the couch. But my feeble arms gave way, and I fell back into the cushion.

"You've got to help me get home," I told Carly Beth. "I thought of a symbol of love. It's at my house."

"Okay. Let's go!" she replied.

"But what about the kids coming over here?" Sabrina asked, swallowing a chunk of Milky Way. "What about the party?"

"You stay here and greet them," Carly Beth told her. "If Steve really can find a symbol of love at his house — and if it works — we'll be right back."

"It'll work," I said. "I know it will."

But I had my fingers crossed. Which made it even harder to climb up from the couch.

Carly Beth saw me struggling. She took both my hands and pulled me to my feet. "Yuck! What are those things moving around in your ears?" she cried, making a disgusted face.

"Spiders," I said quietly.

She swallowed hard. "I sure hope you find something that works."

"Me too," I murmured as she guided me to the door.

Carly Beth turned back into the living room. "Don't eat all the chocolate while we're gone," she called to Sabrina.

"It's only my second piece!" Sabrina protested with her mouth full.

We stepped into the darkness. Some kids in costumes were coming up the driveway, all carrying bulging trick-or-treat bags. "Hey, Carly Beth — where are you going?" a girl called.

"I'm doing a good deed!" Carly Beth replied. "See you guys later!" She turned back to me. "I can't believe you didn't listen to me, Steve. You really look disgusting."

"I can't even wipe the green gobs out of my nose!" I wailed.

Holding me by the shoulder, she guided me toward my house. We crossed the street onto my block. I heard kids laughing and loud music inside the house on the corner. A Halloween party.

As we passed the house, I stumbled over a moving shadow. Carly Beth caught me before I fell. "What was that?" I cried.

Then I saw it scamper silently across the street. A black cat.

I laughed. What else could I do? I had to laugh.

Go ahead, cat, I thought bitterly. Go ahead and cross my path. I couldn't have any *worse* luck — could I?

My house came into view past a row of tall evergreen shrubs. Through the shrubs, I could see that nearly all the downstairs lights were on.

"Are your parents home?" Carly Beth asked, helping me across the grass.

I nodded. "Yeah. They're home."

"Do they know about the . . . uh . . ."

"No," I replied. "They think it's a costume."

As we stepped onto the front stoop, I could hear Sparky start to bark inside the house. I pushed open the door, and the little dog let out an excited *yip* and leaped up at me.

His paws landed on my waist and pushed me back hard. I toppled against the wall.

"Down, Sparky! Please! Get down!" I pleaded in my old man's croak.

I knew Sparky was glad to see me. But I was too feeble for his usual greeting.

"Down, boy! Please!"

Carly Beth finally managed to pull the dog off me so that I could stand up. Then she held onto Sparky until I regained my balance.

"Steve — is that you?" I heard Mom call from the den. "You're back so early!"

Mom stepped into the living room. She had changed into the gray flannel housedress she usually relaxes in at night, and she had her blond hair in curlers.

"Oh, hi, Carly Beth!" she cried in surprise. "I wasn't expecting visitors. I — "

"That's okay, Mom," I croaked. "We're only staying a minute. We came back to get something."

"Don't you love Steve's costume?" Mom asked Carly Beth. "Isn't that the most horrible mask you ever saw?"

"You mean he's wearing a mask?" Carly Beth joked. She and Mom enjoyed a good laugh.

Sparky sniffed my shoes.

"What did you come back here for?" Mom asked me.

"Those black-and-white cookies," I replied eagerly. "You know. The ones you bought me yesterday."

Those cookies were a symbol of love.

Mom had told me how she drove two miles out of her way to buy them for me. She knew they were my favorite cookies in the whole world. And she drove out of her way to buy them because she loves me.

So the cookies were the perfect symbol of love.

I couldn't wait to bite into one. One bite, I knew — and I'd be able to pull off this horrible mask.

Mom's face twisted in surprise. She narrowed her eyes, studying me. "You came back here for those cookies? Why? What about all your trick-or-treat candy?"

"Uh . . . well . . ." I stammered. My brain stalled. I couldn't think of a good reason.

"He had a strong craving," Carly Beth chimed in. "He told me he's been thinking about those cookies all night."

"That's right. I had a craving," I repeated. "Candy bars can't compare, Mom. Those cookies are the best."

"I love them, too," Carly Beth added. "So I came back with Steve. We want to bring them to my Halloween party."

Mom tsk-tsked. "What a shame," she said.

"Huh?" I cried, feeling my heart skip a beat. "What do you mean? What's wrong?"

Mom shook her head. "The cookies are gone," she replied softly. "The dog found the box this morning and broke into it. I'm sorry, guys. But Sparky ate them all."

25

Mom's words sent a cold shiver down my back. I let out a weak moan. And stared down at Sparky.

The dog gazed up at me and began wagging his stubby tail. As if he were pleased with himself!

"You've ruined my life, Sparky!" That's what I felt like screaming. "You greedy pig! Couldn't you save me just one cookie? Now I'm doomed. Doomed to live with this gross, frightening face forever."

And all because Sparky loved black-and-white cookies as much as I did.

Still wagging his tail, Sparky ran over to me and brushed his furry, black body against my leg. He wanted to be petted.

Forget it, I thought. No way I'm petting you — you traitor.

I heard Dad calling Mom from the den. "Have fun, guys," Mom said. She waved to Carly Beth and me and hurried off to see what Dad wanted.

Have *fun*, guys?

I'm *never* going to have fun again, I realized.

Feeling weak and defeated, I turned to Carly Beth. "Now what do we do?" I whispered.

"Quick — pick up Sparky," she whispered back, motioning to the dog with both hands.

"Huh? Do what? I'm never touching this dog again!" I croaked miserably.

Panting hard, his tongue hanging to the floor, Sparky brushed my ankle again.

"Pick him up!" Carly Beth insisted.

"Why?"

"Sparky is your symbol of love!" Carly Beth declared. "Look at him, Steve. Look how much that dog loves you."

"He loves me so much, he ate all my cookies!" I wailed.

Carly Beth frowned at me. "Forget about the cookies. Pick up the dog. Sparky is your symbol of love. Pick him up and hold him against you. And I'll bet the mask will come right off."

"I guess it's worth a try," I said softly. I started to pick up the little black terrier. My back creaked as I bent down. My aching knees cracked.

Please work! I pleaded silently. *Please let this work!*

I reached for Sparky — and he darted through my hands and ran across the carpet toward the den.

"Sparky — come back! Sparky!" I cried, still bent over, still reaching out both hands.

The dog stopped halfway across the living room and turned back.

"Come back, Sparky!" I called in my old man's quivering voice. "Come back, boy! Come back to Steve!"

His stubby tail started wagging again. He stared at me, head tilted, and didn't move.

"He's playing games with me," I told Carly Beth. "He wants me to chase him."

I got down on my knees and motioned to Sparky with both hands. "Come, boy! Come! I'm too old to chase you! Come, Sparky!"

To my surprise, the dog let out a *yip*, ran back across the room, and jumped into my arms.

"Hug him tight, Steve," Carly Beth urged. "Hug him tight. It's going to work. I know it will!"

The little dog felt so heavy in my weak, aching arms. But I held him against my chest. Held him tight.

Held him as tight as I could.

Held him for a long, long time.

And nothing happened.

26

After about a minute, the dog got tired of being squeezed. He jumped out of my arms, bounced over the carpet, and disappeared into the den.

I tugged at the mask with both hands.

But I knew I was wasting my strength. It didn't feel any different. Nothing had changed. The hideous face was still tightly attached to my head.

Carly Beth put a hand gently on my shoulder. "Sorry," she murmured. "I guess each mask is different."

"You mean I need something *else* to get it off," I said, shaking my old, spider-infested head sadly.

Carly Beth nodded. "Yes. Something else. But we don't know what it is."

I uttered a helpless cry. "I'm doomed!" I wailed. "I can't even climb up off my knees!"

Carly Beth slid both of her hands under my shoulders and lifted me to my feet. I steadied myself, leaning on the cane.

And then I had an idea.

"The man in the cape," I croaked. "He'll know what I can do."

"You're right!" Carly Beth's face brightened. "Yes, you're right, Steve. He helped me last Halloween. If we go back to the party store, I know he'll help you!"

She started to pull me to the front door. But I held back. "There's just one little problem," I told her.

She turned back to me. "Problem?"

"Yeah," I replied. "I forgot to tell you. The party store is closed. It went out of business."

We walked there anyway. Well, I didn't exactly walk. I limped and hobbled, feeling weaker and more feeble every second. Carly Beth practically had to carry me.

The streets stood empty, glimmering dimly under the rows of streetlamps. Lights were going out in all the houses. It was pretty late. All of the trick-or-treaters had gone home.

Two dogs followed us down the street. Big German shepherds. Maybe they thought we'd share our Halloween candy with them. Of course, I didn't *have* any Halloween candy.

"Go away," I snarled at them. "I don't like dogs anymore. Dogs are useless!"

To my surprise, they seemed to understand. They turned and went loping across a dark front lawn, disappearing around the side of the house.

A few minutes later, we passed the row of small shops and stepped up in front of the party store. Dark. Empty.

"Out of business," I murmured.

Carly Beth pounded on the front door. I peered into the blue shadows beyond the dusty front window. Nothing moved. No one in there.

"Open up! We need help!" Carly Beth shouted. She banged on the wooden door with both fists.

Silence inside. No one stirred.

A cold wind swept down the street. I shivered. I tried to bury my ugly head in my shoulders. "Let's go," I mumbled. Defeated.

Doomed.

Carly Beth refused to give up. She pounded the door with both fists.

I turned away from the window — and gazed at the alley beside the store. "Whoa. Wait," I called to her. "Come over here."

I dragged myself to the alley. Carly Beth followed. She rubbed her knuckles. I guess they were sore from pounding so hard on the door.

I could see from the sidewalk that the trapdoor was shut. But I led Carly Beth into the alley. We stopped beside the trapdoor.

"It leads into the basement of the party store," I explained. "All the masks and other stuff are down there."

"If we can get down there," Carly Beth whispered, "maybe we can find a way to help you."

"Maybe," I whispered back.

Carly Beth bent down and grabbed the wire handle to the trapdoor. She tugged it up hard.

The door didn't budge.

"I think it's locked," she groaned.

"Try again," I urged. "It sticks. It's very hard to open."

She bent down, grasped the handle in both hands, and pulled again.

This time the door swung up, revealing the concrete stairs that led down to the basement.

"Come on. Hurry, Steve." Carly Beth tugged my arm.

My last chance, I thought. My last chance.

Trembling, I followed her down into the heavy darkness.

27

We huddled close together as we made our way across the basement floor. Pale light from a streetlamp floated in through the open trapdoor.

Across the room, I heard the steady *drip drip drip* I'd heard before. The large cartons stood just where Chuck and I had left them. Three or four of them were still open.

"Well. Here we are," Carly Beth murmured. Her words sounded hollow, echoing softly against the stone basement walls. Her eyes darted around the room, then stopped on me. "Now what?"

I shrugged. "Search through the cartons, maybe?"

I stepped over to the nearest one and peered inside. "This one has all the masks," I told her. I picked up a monster mask covered in bristly fur.

"Yuck," Carly Beth groaned. "Put it down. We don't need another mask."

I dropped the mask back into the carton. It made a soft *plop* as it landed on the other masks.

"I don't know *what* we need," I said. "But maybe we can find something . . ."

"Look at these!" Carly Beth cried. She had pulled open another carton. She held up some kind of jumpsuit. It had a long, pointy tail on the back.

"What's that?" I demanded, stepping around two cartons to get to her.

"A costume," she replied. She leaned into the carton and pulled out another one. A pair of furry tights covered with leopard spots. "The box is filled with costumes."

"Big deal," I grumbled. "That's not going to help me."

I sighed. "*Nothing* is going to help me."

Carly Beth didn't seem to hear me. She leaned over the edge of the box and pulled out another costume. She held it up in front of her. A shiny black suit. Very fancy. Like a tuxedo.

As I stared at it, my face began to tingle.

"Put it down," I said glumly. "We need to find — "

"Oh, *yuck!*" Carly Beth cried. "This suit — it's crawling with spiders!"

"Huh?" I gasped. My face tingled harder. I heard a loud buzzing in my ears. The tingle became an itch.

"Hey, I'll bet this is the costume that goes with your mask!" Carly Beth declared. She carried it over to me. "See? Spiders and more spiders!"

119

I scratched my itching cheeks. The itch was quickly becoming painful. I scratched harder.

"Get it away from me! It's making me itch!" I cried.

Carly Beth ignored my plea. She held the shiny black suit up in front of me, beneath my itching, burning face.

"See? You have the head — and this is the body that goes with it," she said, holding it against me. Admiring it.

"Put it away!" I shrieked. "My face — it's burning! Ow!"

I slapped frantically at my cheeks. My forehead. My chin.

"Owwwwww!" I howled. "I feel so weird! What is *happening* to me?"

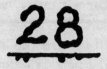

28

"It's burning hot!" I shrieked. *"Owwwwww! What is happening?"*

I grabbed the sides of my face, trying to soothe away the burning pain.

As I gripped my cheeks, the face began to slide under my hands.

I felt it begin to rise. Up, up.

I pulled my hands away — as the old man's head slid over my head. Lifted off. Floated up.

Cool air greeted my cheeks. I took a deep breath of the cold, fresh air.

The craggy old head hovered above me for a moment. Then it floated toward the shiny black suit in Carly Beth's hand.

The head floated down onto the collar of the suit.

Carly Beth let out a startled cry as the suit's arms thrashed out. The trouser legs kicked. The suit twitched and squirmed as if trying to break free.

Carly Beth let go of it and jumped back.

A smile spread over the ugly old face. The suit legs lowered themselves to the floor. The old man performed a little dance, arms flapping, trouser legs hopping.

And then he turned away from us. The head attached to the suit. The trouser legs bent at the knees, he shuffled toward the steps.

Carly Beth and I both cried out in shock as the old man climbed up the steps and disappeared out the trapdoor.

We stood there, eyes bulging, mouths wide-open. We stared at the opening at the top of the stairs. Stared in silence. Stared in amazement.

And then we both began to laugh.

We fell on each other, laughing, laughing till tears rolled down our cheeks.

I laughed louder and harder than I had ever laughed. Because I was laughing in *my* voice. Laughing with *my* face. My *real* face.

The old-man face found its body — and escaped.

And now I was *me* again!

This had to be the best Halloween ever! I had never been so happy in all my life just to have things *normal*.

Carly Beth and I danced down the street as we made our way home. We sang at the top of our lungs. Sang and twirled each other around.

And danced and strutted down the middle of the street.

We were both so happy!

We were half a block from my house — when the creature leaped out from behind a hedge.

It opened its jaws in a broken-toothed roar.

Carly Beth and I grabbed each other and uttered shrill cries of terror.

The creature had bright purple skin that glowed in the light from the streetlamp. Fiery red eyes. A mouth full of broken, rotting teeth. And a fat, brown worm poking out from the middle of its cheek.

"Huh?" I stared at the worm as it bobbed from the creature's skin. Stared at the frightening purple face.

And recognized it.

"Chuck!" I cried.

He let out a hoarse laugh from behind the mask. "I gotcha!" he bellowed. "I got both of you! You should have seen the looks on your faces!"

"Chuck — "

"I've been waiting here. Waiting to surprise you," he rasped. The disgusting worm bobbed up and down in his cheek as he talked.

"You didn't see me grab this mask when I ran out of that store basement," he growled. "I kept it a secret. I wanted to give you a good scare."

"You scared *me* to death!" Carly Beth admitted,

giving him a playful shove. "Now take off the mask and let's go to my house."

"Uh . . . I have a problem," Chuck replied, lowering his voice.

"Problem?"

Chuck nodded. "I'm having a little trouble getting this mask off. Think you guys could help me?"

Add *more*

to your collection . . .

Here's a chilling preview of

GO EAT WORMS!

5

The class bell rang. The sharp clang cut through the rising wind. The rain started to patter loudly against the ground.

"We've got to go in," Danny urged, tugging at Todd's sleeve.

"Wait," Todd said, his eyes on Patrick. "Tell me now!" he insisted.

"But we'll be late!" Danny insisted, tugging at Todd again. "And we're getting soaked."

Patrick climbed to his feet. "I think I've got all the worms I need." He shook wet dirt off the silvery trowel.

"So what is your worm project?" Todd repeated, ignoring the pattering rain and Danny's urgent requests to get back inside the school.

Patrick grinned at him, revealing about three hundred perfect, white teeth. "I'm teaching them to fly," he said.

"Huh?"

"I'm putting cardboard wings on them and teaching them to fly. Wait till you see it! It's a riot!" He burst out laughing.

Danny leaned close to Todd. "Is he for real?" he whispered.

"Of course not!" Todd shot back. "Don't be a jerk, Danny. He's goofing on us."

"Hey — you're not funny," Danny told Patrick angrily.

"We're late, guys. Let's get going," Patrick said, his grin fading. He started toward the school building.

But Todd moved quickly to block his path. "Tell me the truth, Patrick. What are you planning to do?"

Patrick started to reply.

But a low rumbling sound made him stop.

They all heard it. A muffled roar that made the ground shake.

The worm can fell out of Patrick's hand. His blue eyes opened wide in surprise — and fear.

The rumbling gave way to a loud, cracking noise. It sounded as if the whole playground were splitting apart.

"Wh-what's *happening*?" Patrick stammered.

"Run!" Todd screamed as the ground trembled and shook. "Run for your life!"

6

"Why are you so late? Where've you been? In another earthquake?" Regina teased.

"Ha-ha," Todd said bitterly. "Danny and I weren't making it up. It happened again! And Patrick was there, too."

"How come no one else felt it?" Regina demanded. "I had the radio on after school. And there was nothing about an earthquake on the news."

It was nearly five o'clock. Todd had found his sister in the garage, up on an aluminum ladder, working hard on her giant robin. Somehow she had managed to get clumps of papier-mâché in her hair and down the front of her T-shirt.

"I don't want to talk about the earthquake," Todd muttered, stepping into the garage. "I know I'm right."

The rain had ended just before school let out. But the driveway was still puddled with water.

His wet sneakers squeaked as he made his way to Regina's ladder.

"Where's Beth?" he asked.

"She had to go get her braces tightened," Regina told him, concentrating on smoothing out the papier-mâché beak. She let out a loud groan. "I can't get this beak smooth."

Todd kicked dejectedly at an old tire that leaned against the garage wall.

"Look out!" Regina called.

A wet clump of papier-mâché landed at Todd's feet with a plop. "You missed me!" he cried, ducking away.

"So? Where've you been?" Regina asked.

"Miss Grant kept me after school. She gave me a long lecture."

"About what?" Regina stopped to examine her work.

"I don't know. Something about running in school," Todd replied. "How are you going to get this dumb bird to the science fair?"

"Carry it," Regina answered without hesitating. "It's big, but it's really light. I don't suppose you would help Beth and me?"

"I don't suppose," Todd told her, wrapping his hand around the broomstick that formed one bird leg.

"Hey — get your paws off!" Regina cried. "Leave it alone!"

Todd obediently backed away.

"You're just jealous because Christopher Robin is going to win the computer," Regina said.

"Listen, Reggie — you've *got* to tell me what Patrick MacKay is doing for his worm project," Todd pleaded. "You've *got* to."

She climbed down off the ladder. She saw the big worm in Todd's hand. "What's that for?" she demanded.

"Nothing." Todd's cheeks turned pink.

"You planned to drop that down my back, didn't you?" Regina accused him.

"No. I was just taking it for a walk," Todd told her. He laughed.

"You're a creep," Regina said, shaking her head. "Don't you ever get tired of those dumb worms?"

"No," Todd replied. "So tell me. What's Patrick's project?"

"You want to hear the truth?" Regina asked.

"Yeah."

"The truth is, I don't know," his sister confessed. "I really don't know *what* he's doing."

Todd stared hard at her for a long moment. "You really don't?"

She crossed her heart. "I really don't know."

Todd suddenly had an idea. "Where does he live?" he asked eagerly.

The question caught Regina by surprise. "Why?"

"Danny and I can go over there tonight," Todd said. "And I'll ask him what he's doing."

"You're going to go to his house?" Regina asked.

"I've *got* to find out!" Todd exclaimed. "I've worked so hard on my worm house, Reggie. I don't want Patrick the Copycat to do something better."

Regina eyed her brother thoughtfully. "And what will you do for *me* if I tell you where he lives?"

A grin spread over Todd's face. He held up the worm. "If you tell me, I won't put this down your back."

"Ha-ha," Regina replied, rolling her eyes. "You're a real pal, Todd."

"Tell me!" he insisted eagerly, grabbing her by the shoulders.

"Okay, okay. Don't have a cow. Patrick lives on Glen Cove," Regina replied. "I think the number is 100. It's a huge, old mansion. Behind a tall fence."

"Thanks!" Todd said. "Thanks a lot!"

Then, as Regina bent down to pick up the globs of papier-mâché from the garage floor, he dropped the worm down the back of her T-shirt.

7

"I can't believe we're doing this," Danny complained. "My parents said I couldn't come over. As soon as they went grocery shopping, I ducked out. But if they catch me . . ." His voice trailed off.

"We'll be back home in fifteen minutes," Todd said. He shifted gears and pedaled the bike harder. Danny's old bike splashed through a deep puddle at the curb.

The rain clouds had rolled away. But the wind still gusted, cool and damp. The sun had set about an hour before. Now a thin sliver of moon hung low in the evening sky.

"Where is the house? On Glen Cove?" Danny asked, out of breath.

Todd nodded. He shifted gears again. He liked shifting back and forth. It was a new bike, and he still hadn't gotten used to so many gears.

A car rolled toward them rapidly, the glare of its white headlights forcing them to shield their eyes. Danny's bike rolled up onto the curb, and he nearly toppled over. "Why'd they have their brights on?" he griped.

"Beats me," Todd replied.

They turned sharply onto Glen Cove. It was a wide street of old houses set back on broad, sloping lawns. The houses were set far apart, separated by dark wooded areas.

"No streetlights," Danny commented. "You'd think rich people could afford streetlights."

"Maybe they like it dark," Todd replied thoughtfully. "You know. It helps keep people away."

"It's kind of creepy here," Danny said softly, leaning over his handlebars.

"Don't be a wimp. Look for 100," Todd said sharply. "That's Patrick's address."

"Wow. Check out that house!" Danny said, slowing down and pointing. "It looks like a castle!"

"I think 100 must be on the next block," Todd called, eagerly pedaling ahead.

"What are we going to say to Patrick?" Danny asked, breathing hard, struggling to catch up.

"I'm just going to ask him if we can see his worm project," Todd replied, his eyes searching the darkness for address signs. "Maybe I'll act like I want to help him out. You know. Give him a few tips on how to take care of the worms."

"Nice guy," Danny teased. He chuckled to himself. "What if Patrick says no?"

Todd didn't reply. He hadn't thought of that.

He squeezed the hand brakes. "Look." He pointed to an enormous house behind a tall iron fence. "That's his house."

Danny's brakes squealed as he brought his bike to a stop. He lowered his feet to the wet pavement. "Wow."

The house rose up over the broad, tree-filled lawn, black against the purple night sky. It was completely dark. Not a light on anywhere.

"No one home," Danny said, whispering.

"Good," Todd replied. "This is even better. Maybe we can look down in the basement window or find the window to Patrick's room, and see what he's working on."

"Maybe," Danny replied reluctantly.

Todd glanced around. Patrick's house was the only one on the block. And it was surrounded by woods.

Both boys climbed off their bikes and started to walk them to the driveway.

"I can't believe Patrick would live in such a wreck of a place," Todd said, pulling off his cap and scratching his hair. "I mean, this house is a real dump."

"Maybe his parents are weird or something," Danny suggested as they parked their bikes.

"Maybe," Todd replied thoughtfully.

"Sometimes rich people get a little weird," Danny said, climbing on to the porch and ringing the doorbell.

"How would *you* know?" Todd said, snickering. He pulled his cap back down over his dark hair and rang the bell again. "No answer. Let's check out the back," he said, hopping off the porch.

"What for?" Danny demanded.

"Let's just look in the windows," Todd urged, moving along to the side of the house. "Let's see if we can see anything at all."

As they turned the corner, it grew even darker. The pale sliver of moonlight was reflected in one of the upstairs windows. The only light.

"This is dumb," Danny complained. "It's too dark to see anything inside the house. And, besides —"

He stopped.

"*Now* what's wrong?" Todd demanded impatiently.

"Didn't you hear it? I heard it again," Danny said. "Like a growl. Some kind of animal growl."

Todd didn't hear the growl.

But he saw something enormous running toward them.

He saw the evil red glow of its eyes — unblinking eyes trained on him.

And he knew it was too late to escape.

About the Author

R.L. STINE is the author of the series *Fear Street*, *Nightmare Room*, *Give Yourself Goosebumps*, and the phenomenally successful *Goosebumps*. His thrilling teen titles have sold more than 250 million copies internationally — enough to earn him a spot in the *Guinness Book of World Records*! Mr. Stine lives in New York City with his wife, Jane, and his son, Matt.

Dare to Read them All!

Goosebumps®

- ❏ The Abominable Snowman of Pasadena
- ❏ Attack of the Mutant
- ❏ Bad Hare Day
- ❏ The Barking Ghost
- ❏ The Cuckoo Clock of Doom
- ❏ The Curse of the Mummy's Tomb
- ❏ Deep Trouble
- ❏ Egg Monsters from Mars
- ❏ Ghost Beach
- ❏ Ghost Camp
- ❏ The Ghost Next Door
- ❏ Go Eat Worms!
- ❏ The Haunted Mask
- ❏ The Headless Ghost
- ❏ The Horror at Camp Jellyjam
- ❏ How I Got My Shrunken Head
- ❏ How to Kill a Monster
- ❏ It Came from Beneath the Sink!

- ❏ Let's Get Invisible!
- ❏ Monster Blood
- ❏ Monster Blood II
- ❏ A Night in Terror Tower
- ❏ Night of the Living Dummy
- ❏ Night of the Living Dummy II
- ❏ One Day at HorrorLand
- ❏ Piano Lessons Can Be Murder
- ❏ Revenge of the Lawn Gnomes
- ❏ Say Cheese and Die!
- ❏ Say Cheese and Die—Again!
- ❏ The Scarecrow Walks at Midnight
- ❏ A Shocker on Shock Street
- ❏ Stay Out of the Basement
- ❏ Welcome to Camp Nightmare
- ❏ Welcome to Dead House
- ❏ The Werewolf of Fever Swamp
- ❏ You Can't Scare Me!

Available Wherever Books Are Sold.